DEAD LOST

A gripping detective thriller full of suspense

HELEN H. DURRANT

JOFFE
BOOKS

Published 2016 by Joffe Books, London.

www.joffebooks.com

© Helen Durrant

ISBN-13: 978-1-911021-31-5

Prologue

His cigarette was just a stub. He took one last drag and tossed it into the gutter. It had been worth waiting until the shops closed. He'd been given a pile of left-over sandwiches from the café and a passing woman had thrust a carton of hot coffee into his hands. He peered into the hat on the pavement in front of him — about two pounds eighty, he guessed. Not great but better than nowt. There was hardly anyone around on Leesdon High Street now so he might as well head back.

"Hard times?" someone asked.

"The worst, mate. Wife left me, lost my job," he replied without looking up. "But you don't want to listen to my problems."

"Perhaps I can help."

"I don't see how. No one wants to help; don't you read the local newspaper?"

Now he looked up. There was something about the voice . . . but all he could see was a shape standing in the shadows. The man wore a top with the hood pulled low over his face and the zipper done up over his chin.

"I know you," the homeless man said warily.

"And I know you but it's been a while. Not that we bothered with each other much back then."

The homeless man's mouth pulled into a thin line. "I haven't said anything. It's none of my business."

The man in the shadows tutted. "Got to you though, didn't it? One day your conscience will get the better of you too and then I'll be stuffed."

"That won't happen. I'll keep my mouth shut. I have done so far, haven't I? You're safe, I'm safe. Sleeping rough changes a man."

"You call it safe? Living with a load of down and outs in that tented village? Chase Mill isn't as safe as you think. Not now you've got me there too." He had become aggressive.

"I won't blab; that's not my style. Just go. Leave me alone — I'm no threat."

"Perhaps you're right. Perhaps I'll just drive on and forget I ever saw you."

The homeless man relaxed a little. "I won't talk. I don't give a toss what you did." He sniffed. "Life's hard enough. Like I said, living rough isn't easy."

"I've got a lift back to camp. You can come too if you like, there's plenty of room. It's quite a walk back to Chase's. And if you don't mind me saying, your footwear's seen better days."

He shouldn't trust him. He knew he should make some excuse, but his bones ached. It was the constant cold and damp that came with living rough. The homeless man shook his head. "I should wait for Ron."

"We'll pick him up on the way. What do I call you, anyway? I never did know your name."

"Snap. Snap Langton. You?"

"Just call me 'mate.' It'll do for now."

Snap hauled up his tall, thin frame and stretched his arms. He'd been sitting hunched over his hat for the last three hours. He stuffed the sandwiches into one of his coat pockets and the money into the other. The coat was old, ripped and several sizes too big, but it had got him through the winter and that was what counted.

"They've got loads of clothes back at the camp. You should get yourself a better coat," the stranger said.

Snap took no notice. This lift, d'you think he'd drop me by the corner of the mill? Then I'll walk the rest."

"Please yourself. The car's parked just around the corner."

They walked in silent single file down a dark side street. Snap was uneasy. Why would this man help him like this? He must be aware that if Snap chose to, he could really drop him in it. The man was dangerous — a real nasty piece of work. He should have said something to the others. Perhaps he would when he got back. But he'd have to be careful. For the last six months or so he'd survived on his wits and the kindness of others, and that's why he kept his mouth shut. It was safer. Living rough for so long had taught him how to survive. He lived among all sorts, and most of them had a story to tell. He was well aware of the need to stay on his toes, so what had gone wrong tonight? He could have kicked himself.

"Look, mate, I think I'll walk. There're a couple of blokes I need to see on the way," he lied.

The man stopped, turned and stared at him. All Snap could see were his eyes burning in the dark.

"Why Snap? Why do they call you that?"

"You know why."

The man shook his head.

"Because I used to take photos, mate. For a living. Remember? Not any more though, no enthusiasm for it now."

"Got you into this mess, didn't it? But you do have a proper name?"

"Don't use it. I'm not the same bloke now."

"I see."

Snap decided to turn back. He walked away in the opposite direction — fearful. He shouldn't have come this way. The street was dark and deserted. It'd been a long day. He should have gone back to the camp earlier. . .

The first blow struck the back of his skull. It took Snap a moment to register the fact that he'd been hit. Quick as a blink, a searing pain followed in his shoulder. He swung round to clock the bastard. But it didn't happen. The man was holding a machete and Snap staggered back in shock. His arm was gone — the arm he'd tried to hit him with. It lay on the pavement in a pool of blood. He stood, rooted to the spot. He desperately wanted to run, but he couldn't move. The blade came down again, slicing into his chest.

Chapter 1

DS Ruth Bayliss was resolute. "I intend to keep working right up to the end. So don't keep telling me to go home and put my feet up." At the warehouse she was first out of the car, as if to prove her point.

"Just thought you looked a bit peaky, that's all. Pardon me for caring."

She did look pale, thought DI Calladine, yet pregnancy suited her. Her dark brown hair was longer, hanging in a glossy bob to her chin. Apart from the bump, she remained slender. As she approached her thirty-ninth birthday, Ruth Bayliss had taken on the glow that made some pregnant women beautiful.

"I'm fine, so don't worry. I want treating like always. I might be nearly seven months pregnant but I'm neither disabled nor stupid. I'm more than capable of doing the job."

Calladine sighed, and pointed to a huge gap in the front wall of the warehouse. "This is different, though. We've not had one like this before."

Ruth shook her head. "I hope this isn't a new trend. What happened to climbing in a back window and taking whatever's handy? They must have used some sort of heavy equipment to take out half the brickwork like that."

"Ram-raiding, that's what it's called — perhaps they used a bulldozer? One thing's for sure, this place won't be fit for anything until it's fixed. It'll cost a bit too and put dozens of folk out of work while it's lying idle."

"Harrop's Warehouse employs a lot of people in Leesdon. This is a disaster. The knock-on effect will hit the shops, pubs, everything."

Calladine shouted to a worried-looking middle-aged man in a hard hat and pinstripe suit standing by the door. "Mr Harrop! What's it like inside?"

"Bloody empty, that's what it's like. The bastards have taken the lot. All the stock, even the stuff we had in for repair."

"How much stock did you hold? A rough idea will do."

"Nigh on two hundred thousand pounds worth; all small electrical, all portable and easily sold on."

"Can we come in and have a look around?"

"No — not until the surveyor's had a look. Health and safety said to keep people out."

"The CSI folk will need to come in. When you get the nod let me know and I'll get them started," he said to the man. "Bet they don't get anything though," he told Ruth quietly, nodding at a crumpled heap of wire. "This looks like a professional job. Straight in through that fence, then slap, bang, knock out the wall and in."

"There must have been noise surely? There's houses over the way — shall I get Rocco to ask?"

"Good idea, but I believe uniform have tried already and got nothing." He looked up at a CCTV camera that pointed towards the main entrance. "That and all the rest were taken out with an air rifle. That calls for someone who's a bloody good shot. What about the alarm system, Mr Harrop?"

"Wires were cut." The man walked away, shaking his head.

"I can't believe that half a warehouse is knocked down, all the stock stolen, a stream of vehicles is driven up and down the road in the dead of night and no one notices. It doesn't make sense."

"They'll need somewhere big to stash it too." Calladine walked closer to the huge hole in the wall. "This was carefully planned. I hope Mr Harrop is well insured."

"Rocco will see what he can find, but apart from that, all we can do is wait for the forensic report. In the meantime we can keep an eye on the usual outlets; the pubs, local shops and the markets."

"It's a lot of stuff to shift. It won't be sold piecemeal or locally. It'll have been taken to order, mark my words. We'll have to talk to all the staff. This could have been an inside job."

"Your phone's ringing, Tom."

Calladine fumbled in his coat pocket and held the phone to his ear. It was the duty sergeant from the nick.

"Sir, we've had a report of something odd in Dale Lane in Leesdon centre. Only came in during the last half hour. Some kids reckon they've found some clothing in a dustbin, covered in blood."

Calladine shook his head. "They're having us on. Got to be; it's the school holidays, Easter and all that, it'll be some sort of prank."

"That's what we thought too, sir. But we sent a uniformed officer to look anyway. He reported back saying it was no joke. There's a blood-soaked coat and evidence of bloodstains on the pavement too. I told him not to touch anything, just in case."

"Okay, I'll take a look. Did you hear any of that, Sergeant? It's not as if we have anything better to do, is it?"

"What now?"

"Clothing. An old coat covered with blood in a dustbin on Dale Lane, would you believe?"

Ruth Bayliss shivered. "It could be anything. Maybe someone had an accident. Might not even be human blood."

"I hope you're right. Like I said to the officer, school's out so who knows? It could well be a hoax. The little buggers get bored about now. They've finished their Easter eggs and they've still got a few days to kill before the new term starts."

* * *

The PC who'd been sent to investigate stood a good hundred yards away from the bin, busy diverting the public. Calladine coughed.

"It is a bit smelly up here." He nodded at the uniformed officer and went to take a look. Picking up a twig he tentatively lifted the dustbin lid. A swarm of blowflies poured out, causing him to step back. Holding his breath and squinting slightly he edged closer and peered in. The informant had been right; this was no hoax. An old coat drenched in blood lay festering among the rest of the debris in the bin.

Calladine coughed again and jumped back. He led Ruth a few paces from the bin. "It is blood, all over what looks like a man's overcoat."

"So is this a crime scene?"

Calladine looked around at the buildings lining the street. There were one or two shops — a florist and a hairdresser's. He'd been hoping to see a butcher's, which might have explained the blood. "Could be. We should get forensics down here, check things out. I'll ring Julian."

"Don't we have to go through hoops to get someone from the Duggan? And isn't Julian a little too high and mighty these days to be doing stuff like this?"

Calladine shot her a look. Her tone had been light, but he knew she had a point. The entire forensic system had changed — for the worse. Gone were the days when he could simply ring Julian and then pop down to the hospital to see what Doc Hoyle had made of things. The doc was now semi-retired, whatever that meant, and was last heard of working in the medical centre. But the biggest change concerned Julian. He was now *Professor Batho.*

"I'm going to ring him anyway. He won't mind; he's practically family now I've started seeing his aunt." The aunt in question was Amaris (Amy, for short) Dean, Tom Calladine's lover and the owner of Leesdon's very own New Age shop.

"It's a bit grim though, isn't it, sir — this new regime?"

"We have to work with what we've got. DCI Long has been droning on about cost-cutting again, but he was all for outsourcing when it was first suggested."

"And that's another thing — how long is he going to stay DCI? I thought it was a temporary measure, but it's been months now, and it hasn't done his temper any good."

"Something's in the offing. There was a big meeting upstairs last week. It won't be long now before we get someone permanent, mark my words." He just hoped to God it was someone he could work with. He looked down at his phone.

"Julian, it's Tom. Got heavily bloodied clothing in a dustbin on Dale Lane. There's been no report of a crime but we can't just ignore it. We need to know if the blood is human or not. Do you want it?"

There was a protracted silence. Calladine winked at Ruth. He could picture the professor's face and knew exactly what he'd be thinking.

"There is a protocol you know, Inspector."

Calladine grinned. Exactly as he'd thought.

"Yep, I know, but to hell with protocol. I need a team down here ASAP and you know how to organise that." He heard Julian tut. "We're good for the money if that's what's worrying you."

"It's the workload and then the paperwork, Inspector, as well you know. Where are you?"

Calladine told him and hung up. "He'll be here within the hour," he told Ruth, and turned to the uniformed PC. "Stay here and don't let anyone down this lane. I'll get someone from the nick to come down and cordon the place off." He looked at Ruth. "This lane is usually busy; it's a cut-through to the bus station from the High Street. The entire population of Leesdon could have been through here in the last few days."

"There's no CCTV either. If this was done at night, they chose the perfect spot. There's a street light at each end but nothing here."

So someone had planned this carefully. "Fancy a cuppa?" Calladine suggested.

"Have we got time?"

"Yes, Amy's place is just round the corner."

"Will she mind?"

"Not at all. She'll be pleased to see you."

Chapter 2

"You're limping, Ron. Is your leg bad again?" Cerys Powell was ladling out porridge to the inhabitants of Leesdon's homeless 'village,' which consisted of an ever-growing number of tents huddled together on the land surrounding a disused cotton mill.

"It's fine." He sniffed, and handed her his dish.

"If you want to see the doc I can arrange it." Cerys knew his leg was badly infected following a fall. She'd dressed it a couple of times but it had now got to the stage where he probably needed antibiotics.

"Can't see no doc. Got no address." He shuffled off in the direction of his tent, and she shouted at his retreating back.

"Don't worry about that, Ron! We've got a special arrangement. You'll get treatment — pills — and it won't cost a penny."

Cerys knew that Ron wasn't well and that's why his leg wouldn't heal. He'd been hospitalised a number of times due to his drinking, and his liver was shot. He turned back towards her.

"Ain't seen Snap, have you? Only he's been gone for days."

"I'll keep an eye out," she promised. Cerys decided she'd have to get him to the medical centre one way or another. He was stubborn but he wasn't stupid. An infected leg was a serious threat to someone like Ron, who spent his life on the streets.

Cerys took her work at the camp very seriously. She was concerned about all the people who lived there. Not that she looked like a typical do-gooder. Her multi-coloured hair was short and stood out in spikes. Today the spikes were tipped with pink and blue. Her eyes were heavily outlined in black, and her legs were clad in brightly patterned tights, ending in heavy Doc Martens.

The 'village,' as people now called it, was growing bigger every day. It wasn't an ideal place to sleep but it was better than dossing down in the street or on a park bench. It had started life about three months ago when a couple of homeless lads had come here from Manchester and set up in the yard of the old Chase Cotton Mill.

There were about twenty tents now, of various shapes and sizes. They were occupied mostly by men of working age who couldn't get jobs. But there were a few old-timers, men who'd lived almost their entire lives travelling the road, and one or two women who tended to stay together.

Cerys Powell lived with her current man, Eddie Potts, in the village of Lowermill, one of the largest of the Leesworth villages. She was in her final year of a politics degree at Manchester University and Eddie worked for a building firm in Leesdon. He was a local boy and had a flat in Lowermill. Cerys was happy with the arrangement; life in student accommodation was like living in a constant party, really not her thing. And besides, she liked Eddie a lot; he was good fun.

Cerys had imagined that people in the Leesworth villages had a good life. The area bordered the Pennines, and seemed fairly upmarket. But she was wrong. In Leesdon, anyway, life was hard, especially on the large rundown council estate, known as the Hobfield. Anyone who lost their home in that place had reached rock bottom and the only place to go was the 'village.'

Cerys hated the way things were and did all she could to help. She cooked and served the meals made with donations from Leesdon's food bank. She provided as much clothing as she could persuade the residents and charity shops to give her. But it still wasn't enough. There weren't enough helpers for a start. The team of six were mostly only available at the weekend.

In her opinion the local council wanted a bomb putting under it. These people needed homes and it seemed ridiculous to her that a huge building like Chase Mill was standing empty when people had nowhere to go. It could so easily be turned into flats.

"A mug of tea, love," barked a gruff voice. "And make it hot."

"Help yourself from the kettle over there."

"Have you got some food — something good and hot?"

"Only porridge left. You've missed the eggs and bacon. Breakfast was over an hour ago."

"Look, bitch. I want something to eat, and not that slop. Now stoke up that oven of yours and get me a bacon barm."

"You'll get nothing with that attitude," she told him patiently. "We eat at regular times — you know the rules."

"Don't give me that. I've seen you pushing food his way at all times of the day and night." He nodded at Ron.

"He's ill, so I make an exception."

His fist slammed down on the counter. "Well, make an exception for me, little girlie. Or I'll black both those big eyes of yours."

Cerys was shaking. This sort of abuse was rare. The people who used the camp were usually respectful, grateful for the food and the help they got.

"You're not welcome here," she said, almost standing on her toes so she could look him in the eye. "I want you to leave. If you don't, I'll call the police and have you thrown out."

He clenched his fists, and for a moment she thought he was actually going to hit her.

"Sorry." The word was spoken gruffly, as if it stuck in his throat. "I'll wait." He strode away.

A young man smiled at her as he joined the queue. "Hiya, gorgeous. Was that bloke giving you hassle?"

"Not really," she lied. "He wanted a bacon barm and I've finished breakfast."

"So you haven't got one for me?"

It was Eddie making his usual morning visit. At twenty-four, Eddie Potts was a few years older than Cerys. He was tall with an odd sort of beard that only covered the bottom edge of his chin. He had wild red hair. Despite his youth, Eddie Potts had a face that looked lived-in.

"You can have one, Eddie, but only if you make it yourself and don't let anyone see. Then you can give me a hand." She returned his smile.

He nodded at the bread roll Cerys was slicing in two.

"In Nottingham they call them cobs."

"Well, it all depends where you come from. Around here they're oven-bottom muffins."

"That's not a muffin; a muffin's a cake."

"Not in this part of the world, it's not." She handed him a packet of bacon.

"Weird, if you ask me."

"If you're here for the morning, then you can do some clearing-up. Go round and collect any dirty dishes, and while you're at it make sure they're all okay."

"I really came down to give you this." Eddie handed her a small parcel.

Cerys's eyes widened. "Sure it's not for you? You're the one who's into all that online shopping. Me, if I have any money I prefer a wander round the shops."

"No, it's defo got your name on it — see." He flashed the address label in front of her face.

"Put it down there. I'll open it later."

"Go on, open it now. I want to see what you've got. Hope it's not from some strange bloke making a move on you."

He was like a big kid. "Don't be daft. It'll be something to do with this place." Cerys took the package from him and shook it. There was only the faintest rattle. "There's no sender's address," she noted, "and it's not from my mother, not her writing." She peeled away the tape and took a knife to carefully slit across the padded envelope. It appeared to contain scrunched up newspaper.

"What's this?"

"See what's in there. It could be anything."

He grinned. "What d'you reckon — chocolates, make-up? Jewellery?" "Naughty underwear?"

"Hardly. Not wrapped in newsprint." Trust Eddie to think of something like that! Cerys's eyes went narrow as she saw what the newsprint was hiding.

"What is it, Ed? I don't understand."

Cerys had gone pale. She dropped the package and it landed on the food counter. Sitting on a bed of cotton wool were three small, roundish bones. They were perfectly clean and creamy white. Eddie picked one up and looked at it. She watched him as he carefully turned it around in his hand.

"I'm no expert, Cerrie, but I think this is bone. It looks to me like a larger bone cut up into small pieces."

"They're not human though, are they? Why would anyone send me something like that?"

"I'm no expert but they could be human, someone's idea of a joke?"

"Some joke, Eddie. I'm certainly not laughing."

* * *

"I want to see you later," Amy told him. Her voice was more serious than Calladine would have liked. "So no ducking off down the pub or getting embroiled in something at work."

"Do I do that?" Calladine asked Ruth. "Get embroiled, I mean?"

"All the time, and you're in the pub a lot these days too," said Ruth.

"It sounds serious. Are you going to give me a hint? Is it about us?"

"Some of it is. But it's really about a friend of mine who needs your advice. She's aware that we're close and she doesn't know where else to turn," Amy said.

Calladine could see she was concerned. Amy was standing at her shop counter with a pack of tarot cards in her hands, shuffling them as she spoke.

"Don't let me down. She really does need to see you."

"Can't you get an insight from them?" Calladine said, glancing at the cards.

"I can get nothing, which usually means the problem is in a state of flux."

Something told him this woman, whoever she was, would land a whole heap of problems at his feet. "I'll do my best."

"Take three," instructed Amy.

Calladine didn't like it when Amy went all mystical on him. Nonetheless he did as he was told, to keep her quiet.

He watched as she studied the cards. He'd no idea what any of them meant and he didn't want to know, but he could see that Ruth was fascinated.

"There is a woman in authority. You must beware — she sups with the devil."

"What's that supposed to mean? You've just made that up, haven't you?" Calladine shook his head. He didn't have time for this. "You can keep your readings, but thanks for the tea."

Ruth smiled at Amy. "I'll remind him of what you just said when he meets her. Don't take any notice; he's in a bad mood. The day's only just got started but we've got a busy one."

"Try and sort him out for me before tonight." Amy tilted her head to one side and looked at Ruth's belly. "Do you know what you're having? Boy or girl?"

Calladine looked from one woman to the other. These days it was always like this when he was with Ruth. Nothing but baby talk.

"A surprise, for the time being. When it comes to decorating the nursery, then things might change."

"Ah, practicalities."

"If it was me, then I'd want to know." Calladine helped himself to another biscuit from the tin.

"You shouldn't eat so much sweet stuff. You're putting weight on." Amy smacked the back of his hand. "Keep eating rubbish and downing all that beer and you'll regret it."

"I'm fine."

"Physically you're a mess. Look at yourself, for goodness sake." She ran a hand down his belly. "This is in serious competition with Ruth's."

Calladine was offended. He'd always been fairly fit. Granted he was getting older, but recently he'd thought he was looking better than he had in a long time. He put that down to Amy's calming effect.

"I'll try the gym again. But only if you come with me."

"It's food that's the problem, not exercise. I'll give you a diet sheet and you cut out the crap. It's not just your belly, Tom Calladine. You should think about your arteries too."

Ruth broke in. "Shouldn't we be getting back to Dale Lane? Julian will be there by now. Given what he's costing, we shouldn't keep him hanging around."

"Okay." Calladine grabbed a biscuit as soon as Amy turned her back. "She makes them herself," he whispered to Ruth. "See you later! Won't be late, promise. What does this friend want me for — anything heavy?"

"Might be, but we'll discuss it later. And before I forget — Eve Buckley has been in, more than once. She is becoming quite a regular."

Calladine's face clouded. He'd acknowledged the woman and he'd spoken to her, even if only once, but it was enough for now.

"I think she wants to see you. She hasn't said anything; she's far too reserved, but that's what's at the bottom of it. Why not contact her? Meet up? I think you forget sometimes that she is your mother."

"And I think you forget that she was also, until recently, an *absent* mother."

"Not her fault though, was it?"

She had him there. Oh, what was the use? "I will, I promise, when things aren't so busy."

"He won't," Ruth told Amy. "He'll try and wriggle out of it. All he really wants is for it all to go away . . ."

"We'll talk about it later." He nudged Ruth and opened the door.

Once they were outside, Ruth turned to him.

"I thought you were going to try? Meet her family, your half siblings?"

"Not that easy though, is it?"

"You simply take it slow — but not this slow. Until you do something, Eve Buckley is going to keep popping up and one day you'll be pushed into a corner."

"Not me. I won't let it happen."

"What about Zoe? Isn't she curious about her new grandmother?"

"Curious, but willing to wait. This has nothing to do with Zoe."

"How are you and Amy doing?"

"Me and Amy? We're fine, bobbing along — you know."

"No, I don't know. What does that mean exactly?"

"Our relationship is a lot calmer than the one I had with Lydia."

"Lydia nearly killed you. With her it was all fire and passion."

"Oh, me and Amy can get pretty passionate, believe me."

"But you don't live together. You're both far too independent."

"Not me — I'd move in with her like a shot. But this is how Amy wants it." He pulled a face. It was the one aspect of the relationship that bothered him. But she'd made it clear from the start that she wasn't looking for anything permanent. "I stay over and she comes to mine, but most of the time she seems to prefer her own company."

"That's an odd way to run a relationship."

"She's a complicated woman. She values her independence. I don't like it, but I'm kept at arm's length a lot these days."

"All that stuff she believes in; the tarot and the fortune telling. I see she hasn't got any closer to converting you yet."

"A load of bollocks! And I've told her, but still, it's good business. She does well out of that little shop and all those mad ideas, so I leave well alone."

"You can't continue to leave the Eve Buckley problem alone, though. You have an entire family you haven't even met."

Calladine's face hardened. He didn't want to think about it. "I spoke to her that day, you know — the day we sorted the *bucket list* killer."

"But nothing since?"

"You know what it's like."

"I know what you're like. Ring her. She deserves that at least. None of this is her fault, you know. If your mother hadn't wanted you both to get to know each other, then she wouldn't have left you that letter."

He didn't reply.

"And never forget — it was your mother who wrote it, not your dad."

He often wondered about that. Had his father wanted it kept secret? Had he and Freda even discussed it? He'd never know what had happened between them. But Ruth had a point; Freda had written that letter, so she had wanted him to put things right.

* * *

"Inspector! Do not come any closer."

Dale Lane had been cordoned off and Julian Batho stood with a number of CSI people, all suited and masked.

"What do you think, Prof?" asked Calladine from behind the police tape.

"There is a lot of blood on this." Julian held up the garment, now sealed in a plastic bag. "It's most of a man's jacket or coat. I say most because the right sleeve is missing. I'll have to do all the relevant tests and let you know promptly if it is human blood or not. And don't call me 'prof.'"

"Thought you'd like it. Acknowledgement of your new position and all that."

"It was thrust on me."

Calladine couldn't tell if he was joking.

"Did someone have an accident here?" Ruth said. "Maybe they went to hospital."

"A great deal of blood was lost. If it is human blood, then the individual suffered a fatal injury. We've also found blood traces all along the footpath, right up to that corner there. And a splatter pattern against the wall."

"Nasty — if it is human," said Calladine. "Any idea how long ago this happened?"

"Difficult to say — the blood has dried into the fabric. Possibly days."

"Anything else, Julian?"

"The front of the jacket still has the pocket attached. I found this." He held out an evidence bag which held a ring. "It's a valuable piece: antique. I will put the photos and a report on the system by mid-afternoon."

"Back to the nick, then, get the team organised?" Ruth asked.

"Yep, the day's just taken a turn for the worse. Harrop's is puzzling, but this — we don't even know if we have a victim, and if we do, who is he?"

"Or where is he?" Ruth added.

"Naturally I will do a DNA test. There might be something on file. So all may not be lost, Inspector." Julian gave them one of his little smiles.

He was right of course — same old Julian.

Chapter 3

"I had another walk down that road opposite Harrop's, sir. It's weird; no one heard a thing. Well, not what they should have heard. The old woman who lives in the end house says she recalls just one vehicle. A great big heavy thing, she said, thundering up the road about two in the morning. Woke her up. It's just a pity she didn't stick her head out of the window and take a look."

"Get it all written down on the little board there, Rocco," Calladine told him. "And get a statement off the woman."

"Aren't we putting it on the main board, sir?"

"We might have something else for that one shortly." Calladine took a marker and wrote the words 'human blood' at the top. Underneath he wrote the words 'dustbin,' 'coat,' and 'antique ring, Dale Lane.'

"When did this come in?"

"While we were at Harrop's. Ruth and I attended and we've left Professor Batho and his team gathering evidence. The photos and a preliminary report will be on the system later."

"In the meantime I'll check the hospitals," Rocco said. "You never know."

Calladine nodded. If their victim had gone to a local hospital, then Rocco would find him. The DC was good; in fact his entire team were excellent. Simon Rockliffe, or Rocco as they called him, had been with the team on several tricky cases. His input was always first class and he worked hard. But at times Calladine doubted the young man's dedication to his job. He was young and, according to Ruth, something of a looker, so why was he still single? He worried that Rocco gave far too much to the job and an entire aspect of his young life was going to waste.

"Where's Imogen?"

"She got called into DCI Long's office about twenty minutes ago. She's not surfaced yet."

Calladine wondered what Long wanted with DC Imogen Goode. He hoped that Long didn't have any bright ideas about rearranging the teams. Imogen was also good. Rocco was a first class detective and Imogen had top-class skills, particularly in IT. Calladine was the first to admit that he was hopeless, and was impressed by anyone who could type. But Imogen was something else. He hoped Long wasn't proposing to snatch one of his team. Long's wasn't up to much; DS Thorpe was a lazy sod. With Long as acting DCI with CID to take care of, the station was a second team short.

"Did he say what he wanted her for?"

"No, just asked her to go to his office." And here was Long, standing in his office doorway.

"Can we borrow DC Rockliffe?"

Borrow? What did that mean? "As long as you give him back and while we're at it, what have you done with Imogen?"

"You'll see. Just give us ten minutes or so."

Something was going on and it looked like he was going to be the last to know. Well, he didn't have time to speculate now. He had Harrop's to think about, and now the puzzle of the blood in the bin.

"I'm going to have to leave you for a bit," Ruth announced, checking her watch.

"Why — what are you up to?"

"Antenatal appointment at the medical centre. Jake's meeting me there in about ten minutes."

Jake Ireson was the man Ruth had decided to settle down with, after much deliberation. They'd had their ups and downs, mostly due to her need for independence, but it had worked out in the end, and in a couple of months they would have their first child. Jake was a teacher at Leesworth Academy — it had been a good old secondary modern back in Calladine's day. Jake was doing well, and had been promoted to head of English. During the last couple of years, the school had been given a makeover and the last time Calladine had looked it had done well at inspection. Jake was a pleasant man, uncomplicated, and thought the world of Ruth.

"Long's got Imogen and Rocco in his office. What d'you reckon that's all about?"

"Who knows? It could be anything. If it's something juicy, you can give me the lowdown when I get back."

He hoped it wasn't anything juicy; he had enough to think about.

* * *

Ruth had been gone about ten minutes when DCI Long came looking for her.

"Is Sergeant Bayliss here?"

"Antenatal, Brad. Look what's going on? How come you're dragging off each member of my team in turn?"

"It's not me, mate."

Calladine watched as Long looked behind him to check there was no one listening. "You'll find out soon enough. It's how she wants to do things."

"She? As in *she who must be obeyed*?"

"You're spot on there, mate. Don't know how you do it."

24

He closed the door, leaving Calladine more mystified than before. Just who was this *she*?

"There's been a couple of calls for you, sir," Joyce told him. "A woman, but she wouldn't leave her name. Insisted on speaking to you personally. The second time she rang I got the number." She handed him a slip of paper.

"Thanks, Joyce."

It was a Cheshire number and one he recognised. His mother had had it in her book by the phone. Ray Fallon's. That could only mean that Ray's wife Marilyn was trying to reach him — and that spelled trouble. He scrunched the paper up into a tiny ball and threw it in the bin. He had enough on his plate right now.

* * *

"Ruth! Jake! How nice to see the pair of you." Doc Hoyle was coming out of a consulting room at the medical centre. He nodded at her belly. "How's it going?"

"Okay. You know; get a bit tired but nothing I can't handle."

Jake took hold of her hand. "She should put her feet up more. Not that she listens to me."

"Not long now. About two or three months, isn't it?"

Ruth nodded.

"Don't leave it too long before you stop working. Jake's right, you need the rest."

"I'm saving my leave for when the baby comes. But what about you, Doc? How come you're here? What is it you're doing?"

"I'm no longer working in pathology. I'm seeing to the masses again, Ruth. And it's a long time since I did that. When the pathology department at the hospital closed, it was either retirement or something else. This is the something else. I'm doing part-time locum work, and so far it seems to suit me."

"You don't mind GP work, then? You don't miss the cut and thrust of the morgue?" She grinned.

"Yes, I do sometimes. There were never any complaints, no know-it-all patients arguing the toss in the morgue . . . But things changed, well you know that, and I had to go. The idea of putting my feet up for the rest of my time was soul destroying — so here I am."

"You should ring Tom, plan a night out. I know he'd love to hear from you."

"I'll do that. Perhaps we can all get together before the baby comes."

He had a card in his hand; there were people waiting and he had to get on. He called out the name: "Ron Weatherby!" They watched as a punky-looking young woman helped a man to his feet. He was obviously in pain and the doctor went forward to help. "Take him through."

"Someone's got her hands full," said Ruth.

"That's Cerys Powell. She's a great girl," said the doctor. "Cerys looks after the homeless village, the one at the old Chase Cotton Mill. There are others who help out I believe, but she does most of the work."

"I didn't realise the place had taken root. I'd heard about it but I thought they'd all be gone within a few weeks."

"No, Ruth. The sad fact is they've nowhere else to go. They've been moved on many times, forcibly in most instances. But this time they seem determined to stay put at Chase Mill. Cerys is doing her best. She gets food, clothing and blankets, and they trust her. She came here and insisted that those who wanted could register as temporary patients. We have one or another of them in here most days."

"I have to say we haven't had any bother. They're a pretty quiet lot."

"That'll be the Cerys factor. She doesn't want to give the council any excuses to come down heavy."

"Don't forget what I said about meeting up," she reminded him as he left.

* * *

Doc Hoyle went back to his consulting room. Cerys had got Ron seated and was carefully removing the bandage from his leg. She was a gentle sort and he liked that. Though you'd never guess it to look at her in her punk get-up.

"It won't heal and I've tried everything. A couple of weeks ago, Ron fell on some rough ground we're clearing for the vegetable patch. He scraped his shin quite badly."

A vegetable patch. So they were digging in for the duration. That wouldn't please Leesworth Council, who would like nothing better than to close the place and move the inhabitants on.

"I was going to ask the nurse to call in but I think it's gone beyond that."

"I agree. I'll give him some antibiotics. Keep a close eye on things and, if there's no change over the next three or four days, bring Ron back and we'll go from there."

"I ain't going to no hospital." Ron spoke for the first time. "Killed me mother, one of them places did."

Cerys placed a comforting hand on his shoulder. "It's okay, Ron. I'm sure the doctor can fix it." She looked at Doc Hoyle and then back at Ron. "All you have to do is take the pills I give you each day and you'll be as right as rain, won't he, doc?"

Doc Hoyle nodded. Her words seemed to have calmed the man.

"Would you wait for me in the waiting room? I'll only be a minute."

Ron shuffled off, leaving Cerys and the doctor alone.

"I wonder if you'd look at something for me. I'm not ill or anything — it's about this." Cerys placed her package on his desk and unwrapped the newspaper. "This was sent me by post. I got it this morning and I have no idea what it means or who sent it. Eddie, my fella, says they're real bones, might even be human."

Doc Hoyle donned a pair of latex gloves and picked up one of the pieces of bone.

"They've got to be made of some resin or other, surely? It must be someone's idea of a joke."

The doctor looked thoughtful. "This is no joke, Cerys. They're real enough, not resin, but neither are they human. I'd say they were animal bones."

Chapter 4

Imogen and Rocco were looking decidedly sheepish. Ordinarily, Calladine would have asked them why they'd been called away, but that would have to wait. He stood by the incident board holding printouts of Julian's findings. He pinned a lurid photo of the bloodied jacket top right, followed by close-up shots of the ring.

"Sit down, folks, and I'll go through it. This was found in a dustbin on Dale Lane earlier today." He tapped at the image of the jacket. "Julian has confirmed that the blood is human. It wasn't fresh — it'd been there a few days — and there was a lot of it. Given the jacket, we're presuming the victim was male. Either he had a very nasty accident or he was attacked in some way." He looked at Rocco. "Any luck with the hospitals?"

"No, sir, nothing that would match up with what's on the board. There have been no fatalities that would fit the bill either. I rang Leesdon, Oldston General and the big hospital in Manchester but drew a blank with all three . . ."

He paused and Calladine looked up. DCI Brad Long had just entered the room accompanied by a woman Calladine didn't know.

"Continue, Inspector," said Long.

So this was the mysterious female who'd purloined his staff for a sneaky little chat.

"We know from other blood traces found at the scene that the incident happened within a few feet of the bin on Dale Lane. So we have to ask — if he was fatally injured, where is the body? If he isn't dead, why hasn't he sought medical treatment? Until we know the answer we've nothing to go on but this ring." He tapped the board again. "It's distinctive — antique — so it might be valuable. I've printed copies for you. I want you to ask locally, in the pubs, the cafes, the shops on the High Street; anywhere and everywhere you can think of. I will ask the local rag to put something in the next issue along with this photo. With any luck it might jog someone's memory. We need an identity for this individual. Once we know who he is, we can start to build a picture of his life."

At that moment Ruth arrived back from the medical centre. Calladine nodded and gestured to the board. "Our blood in the bin case. The blood is human, so we're looking at serious assault here, or worse."

* * *

"Tom, do you have a minute?"

Brad Long had a smile on his face, Calladine noted. A rare occurrence these days.

"This is DCI Rhona Birch."

Her grip was very firm.

"Pleased to meet you, ma'am."

"You too, Inspector Calladine. Your reputation goes before you — both good and bad. Your team are excellent; I was very impressed, and they speak highly of you."

He made a mental note to buy pints all round later. In the meantime, he was puzzled. What was she doing here?

Long must have read his thoughts. "DCI Birch is joining us, Tom."

He smiled at her but his mind was in turmoil. Could the day get any worse? Granted they'd needed someone, they had done for a while. But why this hard-faced woman? Brad Long's reign hadn't been great, but he could usually be convinced to do what Calladine wanted. He could tell just by looking at Birch that the situation was about to change, and for the worse.

She looked pissed off, and he hadn't even done anything yet. He had her down as a woman who'd managed to climb the ladder in a very male world and wasn't going to give an inch. She didn't return his smile. Rhona Birch was wearing a dark suit, and had a short, severe haircut and no make-up. He guessed she was in her mid-forties. She wasn't Calladine's sort of woman.

"Does that mean you get your old job back, Brad?"

"Yes it does, Inspector," she answered for Long. "Might I suggest that DI Long takes on the Harrop Warehouse break-in? That will free you up to sort this." She nodded at the board.

She may have said 'suggest,' but her tone of her voice meant *I'm calling the shots now and don't you forget it.*

'I want to be kept up to date, Inspector. I expect my DIs to give me regular progress reports. I also like to be involved." She looked around at them all. "I'm far from being a desk-bound officer. I still like to get out there and get my hands dirty."

God help them! Dragging her around would be worse than having a ton weight strapped to his ankles.

"Anyway, don't let me stop you from getting on."

With that she turned and left the room. Brad Long shrugged at Calladine and followed in her wake.

"Do we know anything about her? What did she say to you two?"

"She went through our records with us, sir," Imogen told him. "She wants me to consider a career with Central working in IT with the serious crime unit; you know investigating cybercrime, hacking, that sort of stuff. She reckons it'd be a fast track to a leg up the scale. Said I could make sergeant within a few months."

"She said something similar to me," said Rocco. "But not IT. She wants me to work with the Oldston lot for a while. She says it's a temporary thing, but if I do go I don't see me getting back any time soon, do you?"

So Birch wanted to butcher his team, and was being blatant about it. He looked at Ruth. Would DCI Birch call her in for a little tête a tête? And what about him? "If the offers are serious, then you have to consider them, of course," he said with gritted teeth. He didn't want to lose either Imogen or Rocco, but he wouldn't stand in the way of their promotion.

"We've both said we'll think it over," said Imogen. "But I'm not keen. I like it here."

"So do I, sir," Rocco echoed.

While they were talking, Ruth had taken a call. "Sir! Something a bit odd. I've had Doc Hoyle on from the medical centre. He wants to see you if you've got the time."

"You've just come from there."

"Yes, and we spoke. Everything was fine."

"Okay, the rest of you, you know what you're doing. Ruth, we'll go see what the doc wants."

* * *

"I kept them here. I think Cerys was relieved to be rid of them," said the doctor.

"The young woman I met earlier, the one who brought in the man with the bad leg?"

"Yes, Ruth: Cerys Powell. She's is a major force behind the homeless village — that's the one full of tents in the grounds of the old Chase Cotton Mill. We dealt with Ron, and then she asked him to wait outside. She showed me these." He handed over a stainless steel dish containing the bones. "Not what I expected, I can tell you."

"Just like old times!" Calladine peered at the contents of the dish. "You, us and, well . . . you get my drift."

32

"They are from an animal, in case you're wondering. Cerys has gone back to the village. She was a little shaken, but that's understandable. She has no idea who sent them, but she's obviously upset someone."

"Has she any idea who?"

"No but the village isn't popular with everyone. The people living there show no sign of moving on either. Perhaps this is someone's way of forcing the issue."

"These are the second lot of unexplained body parts we've had today," Calladine quipped.

"I take it the first incident was no joke. The Duggan on it are they?"

"Julian is, despite his new and much exalted position it's still him we call on. There's been a heavily bloodied garment found in a dustbin," he explained.

"So you don't know what it is you're looking at yet. Could simply be an accident."

Calladine wished that were true, but he doubted it. It had all the hallmarks of another gruesome one.

"I'll get a PC to collect this and take it to the Duggan. They might not be human, but it is harassment. Ruth and I will go and see your friend Cerys. It'll do no harm to put in an appearance."

The doc smiled hopefully at him. "Ruth suggested a get-together. Saturday suit you?"

"That sounds okay with me. Do I bring the gang?"

"The more the merrier, and bring that lovely woman of yours too, if you like."

"You're on — the Wheatsheaf? About seven?"

"Fine by me. By the way, a little bird tells me you've got a new face at the nick."

Calladine shook his head. "Haven't we just. Is she someone you know?"

"Only by reputation, Tom, and you need to be careful. Rhona Birch is known as the *hatchet queen;* the one they send in when they want to cull a team. I can't believe they'd be so stupid where you lot are concerned but, you know, them upstairs don't apply the same logic as the rest of us."

The *hatchet queen* . . . he'd have to watch his step. The new DCI had already offered two of his team positions elsewhere. That meant it wasn't Imogen or Rocco that were getting the chop.

* * *

"She hasn't asked to speak to me," Ruth said, when were back in the car. "Why is that do you suppose?"

"Just be grateful, and don't push it."

"It'll be because I was out. I wonder what she'll offer me, if she does call me in."

"Don't sound so thrilled. You're not ready to move on, are you? Are you another one who can't wait to get away from me?"

"No, of course not. Don't be so down about everything. I'm not going anywhere in my state, am I? Imogen and Rocco have no intention of going anywhere either. Rhona Birch is testing the water, that's all."

"Well, I wish she'd go and test it somewhere else. Apart from bumping into the doc, how did you get on at the clinic?"

"Okay. Nothing to report. But do you know what it says on my notes? It says I'm an elderly primagravida. Elderly! Damn cheek."

"What's one of them?"

"Apparently it's a woman who leaves childbirth until way after her first flush of youth."

"You're not that old."

"Well, I know that, but you know what the medics are like."

"But you're doing fine? Healthy enough?"

"Oh yes, fine, positively blooming the nurse said."

"No need to worry then, is there?"

"No, but it was an insult. Elderly!"

They pulled into the grounds of Chase Mill.

"There must be about two dozen tents in the mill yard," Calladine said.

"Not just tents either. There's a shower, a toilet block and a kitchen." Ruth pointed at the clearly signposted portakabins. "This has taken some organising."

"Not forgetting the amount of persuasion it took to get the council to act. It'll have been them who provided all this."

"Come on then, let's go find Cerys."

Chapter 5

A group of people were gathered around the food counter. The smell of cooking floated on the soft breeze, but Calladine doubted they were waiting for lunch. Their voices were raised.

As they approached, a woman called across to them. "It arrived this morning. Scared me half to death. Come on, one of you must know something. It's a bloody joke, isn't it? Well if it is, I don't appreciate it."

A man turned towards Calladine. "Are you the police? Who does something like this?" He shoved a padded envelope at him.

Package number two.

"DI Calladine and DS Bayliss, Leesdon police. Who was this sent to?"

"Me. I'm Drusilla Patton, and this is my sister, Jean. She took delivery from the postman this morning."

"But the packet was addressed to you?"

"Yes, and Cerys got one too, exactly the same."

"Which one of you is Cerys?"

"I am. The doc told you, then?"

"This is two of them now," Drusilla Patten said. "I want to know what's going on. Why we're getting these — these things?"

A third woman put her arm around Drusilla's shoulder. "I'm sure it'll be okay. The police will soon get to the bottom of it."

"And you are?"

"Jean Patten; I'm Dru's sister. I help out here too, whenever I can."

"What about the owner, Damien Chase?" Ruth asked.

"Mr Chase wants rid of us all," said Drusilla Patten. "We did ask him before the place was set up. He said no way."

"So you set up the camp anyway? Wasn't that asking for trouble? It seems reasonable to me that the owner wouldn't want the village here. He's probably got plans for the place. The mill might not have been used in years but all this land must be valuable." As he scanned the area Calladine could quite easily picture a new housing estate here. He was only surprised it hadn't happened sooner.

Drusilla spoke bitterly. "Oh, he's got plans alright. Dozens of posh new houses that the likes of us could never afford. He's a businessman, Inspector, he gives nothing away. But, unfortunately for him, the council are dragging their heels. So while they do we can make good use of the place."

"I went to see him," said Cerys. "I tried to appeal to his better nature. He wouldn't budge, so we dug in. We use the yard, where you see us now. He made sure we couldn't get inside or round the back. He's even put up a fence."

Calladine could see the high wooden fence with razor wire fixed to the top of it. A little excessive, he thought. Still, it wasn't his land.

"Has anyone made Chase an offer for the land?"

Drusilla Patten snorted. "Like he'd tell us, Inspector. All I know is he wants us gone. He makes life as difficult as possible for us. He has his bully boy on site all the time.

Some young bloke who works for Ace Security. He's ill mannered, and often violent."

"Essentially, you're squatting," said Calladine.

"Yes, I suppose we are. But what are we supposed to do? These people have been moved from pillar to post and they deserve better. The council do a bit, like those portakabins, but they're only paying lip service. It's not nearly enough. Turning the mill into affordable flats, or building new ones, would solve a lot of problems around here."

"And the rest of you, what do you think?"

There was a general nodding of heads.

"Are there others who help out?"

"My boyfriend, Eddie Potts, helps from time to time and so do the Slaters and the Gallimores, but only at weekends because they work," said Cerys.

"We'll need their addresses."

"I'll make you a list."

"Are you aware of anyone else who is against the village, apart from Mr Chase? I'm thinking of someone who might gain from frightening everyone off?"

"No one besides Damien Chase — he's the obvious choice, Inspector," said Jean Patten. "If he can get this mill developed, he stands to make a packet."

Calladine would have to find out more about Damien Chase but he doubted it was him behind the bones. He had the law on his side so why resort to these tactics? In the meantime, there was a brown envelope on the food counter identical to the one Doc Hoyle had shown him. It contained three pieces of bone.

"You will catch the bastard who's doing this, won't you, Inspector?"

Drusilla Patton's accent was so refined that her choice of words made Calladine smile.

"I assure you we'll do our level best. Miss Powell, what did you do with the packaging?"

"I threw it in the bin. I'm sorry, I didn't think, and they've already been emptied."

"If it's any consolation the bones are animal," Calladine told them.

A male voice broke in. "Have they come about Snap?"

"No, Ron, they've come about these." Cerys pointed to the box.

"Who is Snap?" said Calladine.

"He's missing, has been all week. He was meant to walk back with me last Thursday but he didn't show up. Like me, he doesn't like walking along that track on his own in the dark."

"Which way do you come?"

"Off the High Street, onto Back Street, then Dale Lane and then we take the track that leads around the back of the mill. It's quicker than walking all the way round, but I don't come that way on my own."

"I thought the back of the mill was out of bounds."

"You shouldn't pay too much attention to Ron," said Cerys. "He gets confused and he still hasn't got the hang of this place. He comes in from over there usually." She pointed to the path that ran alongside the road they'd just driven in on.

It was worth noting that Dale Lane led to a track and then on to the mill. He'd have to have a look. "Thanks, I'll put the word out, and see if we can find him." Calladine patted the man's shoulder.

"Cerys? Could we have a chat in private? We can sit in my car."

Calladine and Cerys walked away, leaving Ruth talking to the others. When they got in the car, he took out a photo of the ring. "I have something I'd like to show you. Do you recognise this ring?"

Cerys took it from him and studied it carefully. "How did you come to take this?"

"Why, do you know who it belongs to?"

"Well, yes, I think I do. I think this belongs to Snap Langton, the man Ron is worried about. Is he in trouble? We haven't seen him in a while. Some of the others have been asking about him, too, but particularly Ron; he asks every day."

"Does he have another name? I take it Snap isn't his real one."

"I can't remember, but I suppose he must have. Everyone calls him Snap because he used to take pictures before he joined us. I'll get his file, that'll fill in the gaps."

Calladine wrote the name down in his notebook. "Is there anything about him that makes him easy to recognise? Any distinguishing marks?"

"He has a scar, quite a livid one, on the inside of his right forearm. He fell and cut it badly on some glass about six months ago — well, that was what he told me. It needed stitches."

"Which hospital? Do you know?"

She shook her head.

Calladine handed her a card. "Here's my number. Anything you hear, anything you find out about Snap Langton, let me know. Particularly if he turns up."

"Is he in trouble? It's not Snap sending those bones, is it?"

"I doubt it. I think Snap has met with an accident, Cerys, a few days ago. Whether the bones are connected in some way, we've don't know."

"Can I tell Ron?"

"Not yet, not until we know for sure what happened to him. Let's just keep him as missing for now."

"What do you think the bones are all about, Inspector?"

"I've no proof, but if I had to hazard a guess I'd say someone was trying to frighten you off."

"That could be anybody. Most folk ignore us. Some try to help, but I'm sure a big part of Leesdon's population would be only too glad to see the back of us."

"Anyone in particular spring to mind?"

"Not really. We get grief from the lads off the Hobfield most nights; stone throwing, shouting abuse, that sort of thing."

"I'll have a PC keep an eye on you. Do you have a photo of Snap? And also anything belonging to him, anything we might get a DNA trace from? A comb or toothbrush, perhaps."

"I'll get you Snap's file. I take some details when they arrive and I take a photo. His personal stuff is still in his tent. Do you want me to see what I can find right away?"

"Yes, but keep it low-key. I don't want this getting out just yet. I'll speak to the others."

He watched Cerys hurry away. He was impressed with her thoroughness. He returned to the group and began passing his cards around.

"If you receive anything else, you must contact us straight away. That's any more parcels, letters, anything at all."

"When will you tell us what's going on?" Drusilla asked. "Got us all spooked it has. A homeless camp in Stockport got sent a load of dead rats. It was in the paper, I remember reading about it. But this tops even that, I'd say."

"We'll let you know the minute we find out anything. I'll take the box with me and hand it over to the forensic team." He took a large plastic bin bag from behind the counter, donned a pair of latex gloves and carefully put the packet inside.

Calladine and Ruth walked back to the car, and minutes later Cerys joined them.

"Snap's record and his comb. Will that do?"

Cerys dropped it into the evidence bag he held out. "I'll be in touch," he said.

Once she was out of earshot, Calladine turned to Ruth. "What do you think?"

She pursed her lips. "The blood. It looks highly likely that it belonged to one of them, most probably Snap Langton. You do realise that this could be just the start? It looks to me as if someone out there wants rid of them, and are prepared to go to any length to do it."

"I hope you're wrong, Ruth."

"Are we going to the Duggan?"

"Julian should have the other lot by now. We'll drop these off and have a chat. Then we must take a closer look at the route these people use, particularly that track."

* * *

"Tom! Ruth. You have another one? Someone's been busy."

"Busy and meticulous. These bones have been very carefully prepared."

"Carefully prepared, once they'd been harvested . . ."

Ruth shuddered. "They're not apples off a fruit tree, Julian!"

Julian raised his thick, dark brows.

"It's just a word. Whoever acquired these has gone to a great deal of trouble. The flesh was pared off and the bones were chemically treated. Are these connected to the incident with the blood?"

"We don't know," said Calladine. "We're hoping that's something you can tell us. There's nothing to suggest they are, except for my gut feeling. However, the bones are linked to the tented village in Leesdon and the blood might be too. Investigations ongoing. If you haven't already seen it, that's where the ever-growing number of the area's homeless is currently living. The blood might have belonged to one of them, but the rest of him is still missing. One of the helpers recognised the ring you found in the coat pocket. The bones? I've no idea where they fit in. But both packets were sent to folk who help out there."

"I see. Someone has a problem with the whole outfit."

"It's possible. Given the bones have been treated in some way, can you tell how long since they were — er — harvested? A rough idea will do for now."

"It's impossible to say from just looking at them. They could be old; then again they could have been cleaned and cut up a week ago. I'll know more when I start the tests."

"You are absolutely sure that they aren't human bones, aren't you, Julian?" Ruth asked.

"They are definitely not human," he told her. "I can see that by looking at them."

Ruth was relieved but still mystified. Why would anyone go to all that trouble?

"You look almost disappointed."

"Believe me I'm not, but I am puzzled. What sort of bones are they?"

"They're animal of some kind. These have been taken from the long leg bone, the femur. I can tell they're animal because they are thicker than a human's. They've possibly come from a cow or a horse, but I am not a vet!"

"Scare tactics?" Ruth suggested.

"Possibly. I used to collect animal bones myself as a lad, I'd clean the skeletons of animals I found in the wild. I had quite an assortment; skulls of foxes, bird skeletons, even a complete badger."

"That's just gross, Julian!" said Ruth.

"Will it take long, the testing?" Calladine asked.

"I doubt there'll be much to find — no fingerprints anyway."

"Knowing what animal they came from might help further down the line. The boxes and packaging they came in are all here. And will you see if you get anything from this?" Calladine handed over the evidence bag containing Snap's comb. "It might have belonged to the man whose blood we found. We need a positive ID."

"I'll prioritise the blood. I should have something for you by Thursday."

"Thanks, Julian. It's all we've got to go on."

"The coat is old. Yes, it was covered in blood, but the fabric beneath that was also threadbare; ripped and stained. Going by that, your notion that it belonged to a homeless person holds water, Tom."

"Maybe it was ripped during the attack . . ." said Calladine.

"How's your new leader?"

"So, news of the hatchet queen has reached you, has it? She's going to be a first-class pain in the arse, that's how. I'd never met the woman before today, but already I dislike her. She's trying to poach my team. Have a word with your Imogen, will you? The woman had her in the office for a good fifteen minutes, talking alternatives to Leesdon nick."

"I know — she rang me. That's how I know about her."

"Imogen's not thinking of taking her up on that stupid offer, is she?"

"The offer wasn't stupid. Imogen is talented, you know that. But no, she doesn't have any intention of leaving you."

"And don't go persuading her otherwise! Imogen's good, and we need her. *I* need her," Calladine said.

Julian disappeared into his lab. "I'll be in touch. Imogen and I might even make it on Saturday. Bring Amy along, and we'll have a catch-up."

They made for the car. "There's not a lot we can do until Julian's results come in, is there?" said Ruth.

"Lightweight."

"I *am* not, but I am tired."

"I'll drop you at home and then I'll go back to the nick. The team can get some background on the helpers and see if we've got anything on Snap Langton."

"Not under that name we won't."

"You never know. Nicknames do get listed on the records."

Chapter 6

"The DCI's brought in a crew off the Hobfield for the Harrop job," Rocco told him when he got back to the nick.

"She's barking up the wrong tree there. It was an inside job. That stock was moved out weeks before Monday night, mark my words."

"That's what I think too. No noise of heavy traffic on the night of the break-in."

Calladine nodded. Rocco was smart; he'd worked it out.

"So why didn't she listen? Why raid the Hobfield?"

"A bunch of lads were selling stuff cheap, small electricals from Harrop's list. She's interviewing them now. They won't say where they got them so, as far as the DCI's concerned it's all cut and dried."

"Well, it's not. Now she's rushed in without thinking and made a balls-up of it. She has no idea what makes that estate tick. The last thing we need is her getting the scroats off the Hobfield all riled up. We've got quite enough to do."

There was a shout from the office.

"DI Calladine! Can I have a minute?"

He wondered if she'd heard him. Was this a bollocking for speaking out of turn, or time for his little pep talk? Calladine shook his head at Rocco, stuffed his hands in his trouser pockets and entered the office.

"Close the door behind you." Far too severe looking. Calladine didn't like women in positions of power who tried to be like men, and DCI Birch was doing just that, from the masculine haircut to the heavy shoes.

"Sit down, Inspector." Calladine pulled up a chair and sat facing her.

"What are your plans for the future?" She tried to smile but failed. Her wide mouth made a thin line and the frown came back. This woman didn't like him. "For example, where do you see yourself in five years' time?"

The words, *none of your bloody business* sprang to Calladine's mind, but he bit back the words. Instead he said, "I imagine I'll still be working, ma'am, still catching criminals and murderers and doing my best to keep Leesdon's streets safe."

"Not particularly ambitious, is it?"

"Personally I think it's worthwhile. I do a good job. I have a good clear-up rate and there's been no complaints."

"Complaints, no . . . but some cause for concern."

Calladine looked back at her long and hard. What was this?

"What are you trying to say? Exactly who has concerns, ma'am?" Surely it couldn't be a member of his own team, so that only left Brad Long and his cronies. Long had been running the place for the last few months, but he had no cause to complain about anything.

"The Chief Superintendent, Inspector."

She delivered the words with a distinctly satisfied look. He hadn't seen that one coming. The chief worked from Oldston nick and, as far as Calladine was concerned, he could stay there. Interaction between him and Leesdon was rare. So why in the world would the chief be interested in him? Calladine racked his brain. What could he have possibly done to attract the chief super's attention? But more to the point, what did it mean for Calladine's future with the force?

"Ray Fallon is in court next week."

Calladine blinked. Him again! How long was this nonsense about his cousin going to go on for? He wasn't even really Calladine's cousin by blood, as he'd found out recently, but he wasn't going to explain that to this woman. "Yes and the bastard's up for murder."

Birch tutted at his language and then tried to smile again. She was deliberately baiting him. Well, he wasn't going to give her the satisfaction. Nonetheless his stomach did a flip. Fallon was his Achilles heel. He should have realised that his damn cousin was at the root of this. His mind was racing. He'd done everything right, all according to the book. It had been Calladine who'd gathered the evidence that would finally convict Fallon. So what had happened to cause 'concern?'

"Fallon has hired a top-notch, very expensive brief."

Calladine shrugged. "Exactly what I would have expected. He's always got off in the past and he imagines he can do the same thing this time. But there is no denying the evidence. He won't wriggle out of this one so easily."

Calladine knew that Fallon shouldn't wriggle out of this at all. The evidence was irrefutable.

"That's where you could be wrong, Inspector. There is every possibility that he will."

Calladine couldn't believe what he was hearing.

"The chief would like you to consider a period of extended leave for the duration of the case."

Calladine shook his head. "Absolutely not! I'm not giving up my job just because that slimeball has hired some fancy lawyer."

"It's not about the lawyer; it's your relationship with Fallon. And you'll be called to give evidence. You will need time off anyway, Inspector."

"One or two afternoons, tops. There's no way I'm going on leave, extended or otherwise."

"I was hoping to persuade you. The chief is worried that during the case your position on the force — as the officer who provided the evidence against Fallon — will be compromised."

"I don't see how."

"The defence will suggest that you had ample time to fix the evidence — plant it; the blood on the flowers for example."

Calladine was astonished.

"You were at the same funeral—"

"Because I was burying my own mother, for God's sake! And Fallon was there because she brought him up. He was her aunt: family!"

"Nevertheless you were there and you had access to the body in the boot. And you had access to the flowers."

Calladine couldn't believe they were serious. "So I crept out of the church when no one was looking, did I? I went to that thug's car, lifted the boot, helped myself to blood from a dead body — a body, I should point out, that I had no idea was there, and daubed it all over an arrangement of roses? I did all that and no one saw. I was the principle mourner! Are you telling me that no one noticed when I ducked out for a while?" He stood up, ready to leave. "You seem like a bright woman; surely you see how ludicrous that is?"

"Nonetheless, it will plant some seeds of doubt in the jury's minds. You also knew the owner of the care home very well. You did arrange for her to have some of the funeral flowers."

"Because it was pissing down and they'd have been ruined outside!"

"Don't use that language with me, Inspector."

But Calladine wasn't listening. He was already out of the door and halfway down the corridor.

48

He was seething. He'd no idea what was going on. And how come Rhona Birch was so knowledgeable about every detail of that day? Even more intriguing, how come she knew what Fallon's defence team intended to do with that detail? He was going home. He needed to think.

* * *

Calladine sat in front of his sitting-room fire with a scotch in his hand. Amy had said she wanted to see him but he wasn't in the mood. All he wanted to do was get drunk, go to sleep and forget the whole damn thing. Birch had annoyed him to the point that he'd be poor company anyway. She'd put forward Fallon's defence as if she believed it herself. Surely, everyone in the nick knew him better than that? As much as he hated the man he had not fitted him up, tempting as it might have been. So why the questions about his integrity now?

There was a knock on his front door — Amy, he presumed. He'd have to tell her, perhaps arrange something for tomorrow. But the person standing on his doorstep wasn't Amy. It was Eve Buckley.

"Can I come in?"

Without a word Calladine stood aside to make way for her. What was the use? He couldn't hold off all this family stuff forever.

"I'm sorry to call unannounced. To be honest I've been plucking up the courage to come round for ages."

She looked as smart as ever. Her dark hair was neatly styled, her make-up perfect and she was wearing a pair of well-cut denims and a shirt. She certainly didn't look like a woman in her early seventies. In fact, on a bad day he probably looked older than she did — and she was his mother! The thought made him smile. Eve Buckley was so utterly different from Freda, the woman who'd raised him and who he'd always believed was his mother.

"Is it a bad time?"

"Work problem."

"You look ashen. Is it a major problem?"

"Big enough. A new DCI who's just ruined my day."

"I doubt I can help with that, but I might be able to cheer you up a little. I'm here because of tonight. I know it's short notice but nothing was arranged at home until this afternoon. It's Sam's birthday — you know, Samantha, my daughter, your—"

"Yes, I know who she is."

"We're having a small do for her. Nothing fancy, just nibbles and wine, about nine tonight and I'd love you to come. Bring your daughter, if you wish."

"Zoe . . . Perhaps next time." It was too soon to involve Zoe at this point — too many questions he couldn't answer. "Her and Jo, her partner, are up to their eyes decorating their house. And I really don't feel like socialising after the day I've had." He could see from her face that Eve wasn't going to be fobbed off with excuses.

"But you have to come. Bring that lady friend of yours, the one I met at the art exhibition; the one with the lovely shop."

He didn't have the heart. It had taken a lot of courage for Eve Buckley to come here, and that made her much braver than he was. There was no way he'd have gone knocking on her front door, mother or not. Anyway he had to take the plunge one day and he would have Amy at his side for moral support. He nodded. "Okay, I'll ring her and arrange it. About nine? At yours?"

Her smile revealed her perfect white teeth. "Yes. You know where we live."

Indeed he did. His birth mother lived in some splendour on a hillside abutting the Pennines on the Huddersfield road.

She looked around. "I like your home. It's like you, in an odd sort of way."

"You mean it's old and tired."

"No, not at all."

Now he'd embarrassed her, fool that he was.

"What I mean is, it's a home, a real home, log fire and all."

"I like it. I live like I've always lived. My parents' old house is only a few doors up. I was raised on this street."

She was gazing at him. What was going through her mind, he wondered. Was she thinking how different both their lives might have been if she'd kept him?

"We still haven't had that talk . . ."

"We will, but not tonight."

Eve Buckley nodded. "See you both later, then. Dress is casual. Don't go to any trouble."

Calladine wondered if that meant the Buckleys hosted formal evenings too. If they did, and he was ever invited, he'd be a real fish out of water.

"Later, then." She reached forward and kissed his cheek.

It was a natural sign of affection from a mother, but for some reason it rattled him. He didn't know how to respond. "I must ring Amy. Let her know about the change of plan."

"Don't worry. It'll be fine."

Would it, though? Eve, her children and God knows who else. He'd be right out of his comfort zone.

As soon as she left he called Amy. "I'll see your friend tomorrow. In the meantime, get your glad rags on and I'll pick you up about eight thirty."

Amy didn't sound put out. In fact she seemed quite pleased that he was finally making an effort where Eve was concerned.

Showered and dressed, Calladine rang Ruth and told her about his talk with Rhona Birch. "I think she actually believes that's what I did." He was becoming angry again.

"Don't be daft. It's all in your imagination. She's just playing devil's advocate. She's telling you what the defence will make of it, and she's right. You know that Fallon will hire the best. You said as much yourself."

"They want me to go walkabout for the duration. That can't be right. It's hardly supportive, is it?"

Ruth went silent.

"Come on then — what's going on in that shrewd head of yours?"

"I'm just wondering what would happen if he did actually get off. It would make your position at the nick rather difficult."

"That's putting it mildly. If Fallon gets off because the jury believes all this bullshit, then my career is stuffed. Folk might really think I tried to stitch him up and came off worst."

"Look, it's got a long way to go yet so calm down. Go meet Amy and enjoy yourself. It's about time you hobnobbed with Eve and her crowd."

Chapter 7

With only a sliver of moon the night was almost pitch black. Just how he liked it. But he'd still have to be careful. During the day he could do nothing — too many people knew him and too many eyes watched. To do what he needed to do, he had to be alone. The camp attracted attention. It wasn't just the homeless; others came too. All day and after work there were people bringing stuff — food, clothing and bedding for the homeless. Stupid, deluded fools. He needed them to stop. He needed the camp to disappear. He needed this place to be quiet again.

He hid in the shadows on the street leading to the camp. At one end was a scarcely used narrow track that ran alongside the mill fence. No longer maintained, it had huge ruts in the perished tarmac and the fence was full of holes. Drivers had more sense than to come this way. But his prey used it all the time. It was a shortcut and led in to the rear of the mill via a hole in the fence. They got into the camp by moving a couple of loose fence panels in the huge wooden barricade Chase had had put up.

He was coming. The man checked his watch. Always the same time, every night. He watched from the shadows as the vagrant shuffled along, limping. He was short and his head bent forward as he took care with his footing. There were no streetlights along here. All he needed was a couple of minutes; that's all it would take. He called out. "Got a light?" He watched the man stop in his tracks and look around. "Over here! Out of the wind."

"Do I know you? I do, don't I? It is you. Snap said you were a bad 'un."

"I just want a light!" There was a low muttering and then the homeless man shuffled towards him. His shoes were too big and he was almost buried in the long coat he was wearing. "Did Snap tell you anything else?"

"He saw you. He said you were dangerous. You're the reason he left. He said I was better off not knowing it all, but I worked it out. He had nightmares and shouted out in his sleep. I told him what to do but he was a fool." He held a lighted match to the man's cigarette. "What you called anyway?"

"You know my name. Snap will have told you but if you can't remember, then 'mate' will do. What did you tell him to do?"

The homeless man peered up at the hooded face but it was hidden in shadow. "I told him to forget it."

"I want you to help me with some stuff I've been given for the camp. It's just down here."

The homeless man padded along after him.

It was almost too simple. Homelessness must addle their brains. Everything was going like clockwork. Snap hadn't realised the danger, and neither would this one. The element of surprise — it always worked.

"Cop hold of that." He pointed to a dark bundle lying on the pavement by a builder's skip.

As the homeless man leaned over, his arm extended, the man lifted a machete that had been hidden under his top. He took aim and swept it down hard with a single powerful stroke. The blade sliced into flesh just below the shoulder. The vagrant lurched forward and fell onto the road, his partially severed arm hanging at his side. The man repositioned and struck again, this time thrusting deep into his chest. It was done.

He stared down at the bloodied mess on the road. It had been a good, clean kill but he'd have to clean up. He disappeared into the shadows for a moment and returned with a wheelbarrow. He manhandled the body onto it with some difficulty. He threw the bundle containing a crowbar and his machete on the top and made his way, nice and steady, to his special place.

He'd been watching everything and everyone for a long time now, and one night he'd come across this place. It had proved very useful, and it was where he'd put Snap. He, and now this one, would remain hidden forever. Within a few minutes he had reached an open patch of rough ground at the rear of the mill on the other side of the fence. A manhole cover was almost hidden by a grassy embankment. It led down into the sewers.

He knew others used it too. One night a few weeks ago, when he'd been exploring, he'd seen someone, a man with a large bundle — it must have been a body — and watched him shove it down this hole. These days, whenever he removed the cover the smell of death made him sick. He never looked down into that black hellhole. He imagined faces, screams. The hole in the ground could keep its secrets.

He tipped the body onto the dirt. Then he used the crowbar to remove the manhole cover. He rolled the body to the edge and pushed it down. The smell choked him, making him cough. One more down there now. He wondered who was responsible for the others. Whoever it was, he'd found the perfect place. He closed the manhole, scraped soil and weeds over it and threw the crowbar and machete into the barrow.

He wheeled it through a hole in the fence. Some of the others used it too. The useless security firm Chase employed had never noticed it. He pushed the barrow to an outhouse at the back of the mill grounds. It was one of many stashed in there along with a number of sacks, trucks and other stuff that had ceased to be of any use. He wrapped his tools in the large black sheet of cloth and carried the bundle back along the way he'd come.

It had started to rain, so he walked briskly back to the skip. There was a pool of blood on the pavement where he'd dealt with the vagrant. It would probably get washed away. But he didn't want to take the risk. The last time he'd chanced things, it had all gone wrong. He ripped off a large piece of the black sheet and tried to mop up the blood. It wasn't particularly effective but it would have to do. The rain had turned into a torrent — it would finish the job for him. Satisfied, he threw the bloodied rag into the skip and went on his way.

* * *

They pulled into the driveway of the Buckley residence. "We haven't got her a card or anything," said Amy.

"She won't mind."

"Just look at this place; it's enormous. How many bedrooms d'you reckon it's got?"

"Too many for comfort, as Freda would have said. She was dead against heating empty space. To her a big house just meant big bills."

"You miss her, don't you?"

"Of course I do. She was my mother."

"And Eve?"

"I've yet to decide."

Calladine adjusted his tie and looked around at the mansion. It had probably once been some rich mill-owner's house. There were lights everywhere, strung from the trees, around the front, and all down the drive. He could see that it had a large garden. The Buckleys had done well. The pharmaceutical business was obviously lucrative.

"I really didn't want to come, you know."

"Don't be such a stick-in-the-mud. It'll do you good."

"A bad day at work. A case going nowhere. I should be at home, thinking."

"This will take your mind off things. It's just what you need and it'll help your brain work better."

"It could certainly do with something." He could tell Amy was looking forward to this evening. She was all bubbly and she'd dressed up for the occasion. She had a unique style, slightly bohemian, colourful and flowing. The dress she wore tonight was low cut. It draped elegantly to her ankles, around her curving figure, revealing a tantalising glimpse of bosom. She had already mounted the front steps and was ringing the bell. Perhaps she was right; a change of scenery might help. But if it didn't, there was always the booze.

"Come in! I'm really glad you came, both of you," Eve Buckley took hold of Amy's hand and led them inside. "I want you to meet everyone. The only one missing is Simon, my son — my other son. He's in Rome, firming up a deal."

Calladine could see Amy's eyes flickering over the expensive furniture, the antiques and the paintings that adorned the walls. The house reeked of money. The inside was as impressive as the exterior. God knows who would be there. Most of Leesworth's 'who's who,' he imagined. Fifty or so people were milling around, chatting and drinking.

"What would you like to drink?"

"Red wine, please," said Amy.

"A scotch would be fine." Calladine was fiddling with his tie again, feeling suddenly uncomfortable. These were not the kind of people he usually mixed with. They were a long way from the Wheatsheaf, and right now he was nervous, needing the support of alcohol. The party had seemed no big deal when it had been mooted, but now he was here, he felt very different about it.

"You've met Sam, haven't you?" said Eve.

Indeed he had. This could be tricky. How would she react? He shuffled in increasing discomfort as the woman fixed him with a stare.

"Inspector Calladine . . . Tom." Her eyes twinkled. "The last time we met, you thought I might have killed someone, as I recall."

"Oh, not really," said Calladine.

"He did." Samantha Hurst turned to Amy. "He thought I'd killed my lover, Tariq Ahmed. Rubbish of course, but for a moment there he must have had his doubts. Tariq and I worked together at the hospital in Manchester."

"That's history now. It was a difficult situation."

"Indeed it was. You knew who I was, but I'd no idea about you." She turned to Amy again. "It's a problem being a detective when family is involved."

Calladine didn't know how to take her. Was she being serious or making fun of him?

"Are you still working there?" said Amy.

"Yes — and because of what happened I got a leg up. Not that I wanted it, but you can't refuse what is given, can you?"

"Happy birthday, by the way."

"Thank you. I told Mum all this wasn't necessary but she's a law unto herself, as you'll soon come to realise."

"Good of her to invite us."

"Look. This is awkward — for you and for me. Simon stayed away deliberately because he can't hack it. When he found out about you, he was shocked. Ma told us everything. She held nothing back and she made it quite clear to both of us that you are as much her child as we are. She fully intends to 'dovetail' you, as she puts it, into the family."

Calladine blinked. Shaking his head, he looked at Amy. "I've never been 'dovetailed' before."

"It isn't funny, Tom. This is a big upheaval for us and for you. Ma means you to become one of us, whether you want it or not. She's determined, protective and her kids are her whole life. I should warn you that this also extends to the grandchildren. You won't get away with keeping your Zoe out of the picture for much longer."

Samantha moved away to talk to the other guests. Calladine whispered to Amy, "Eve Buckley, the matriarch. And she comes across as so sweet and gentle."

"I'm sure she is. She's a very nice woman and you're a lucky boy. More scotch?"

"That table over there is awash with the stuff. Go see what you can do, girl. A large, single malt from the Isles would go down very nicely."

Calladine looked around. He recognised one or two of the other guests — the local MP and a couple of blokes from Leesdon council. He was tempted to go and ask them about the tented village, but then he spotted someone: Rhona Birch. What in hell's name was *she* doing here?

He watched Amy cross the floor with the drinks. "You're miles away. What's up?"

"That woman over there — she's my current pain in the arse," he whispered. "I can't work out how she'd know Eve."

"Perhaps she doesn't. Maybe she came with someone who does."

Of course. That must be it.

"Him over there, for example." Amy gestured at a man in a dark suit. He was tall with dark, receding hair and had been standing with his back to them. The man turned round and Calladine nearly choked on his whisky.

"It gets even worse! That's the chief super." He downed the whisky and grabbed Amy's hand. "It's time we left. There's no way I can make small talk with that pair. They're after my head — they both are."

"Stop being a drama queen, Tom. We've only been here five minutes. What will Eve say? All we have to do is keep out of their way."

But that was easier said than done. Eve was calling to him.

"Tom! There's someone I want you to meet. My brother. I haven't told him much about you, only that you exist, so he's dying to get to know you better. I have no intention of keeping you a dark secret any longer."

She ushered Calladine closer to the chief super. A quick look around confirmed that Birch had left him for the moment.

"Edwin, this is Tom."

Calladine could think of nothing to say. The man was smiling at him — smiling! He was holding out his hand. "Inspector Calladine — Tom. I'll not pretend. This entire thing came as a huge shock, particularly when Eve finally told me who you were. And that was only this afternoon, after she'd invited you here."

I bet it came as a shock, Calladine thought. Now what would he do about sidelining him during Fallon's trial?

"I'll leave you to it," said Eve.

The super waited until she was out of earshot. "Eve is older than me. I reckon she must have got pregnant with you while I was still in primary school. I never knew. I didn't know your father either. Still, now she's putting things right. I have to say, finding you has given her a new lease of life."

Calladine said nothing. He was out of his depth. During his entire career he'd exchanged perhaps a word or two with this man. And he felt stupid. Why hadn't he put it together? Edwin Walker: the clue was in the name. But he could never have imagined anything as ludicrous as this. The chief super — the man who had overall control of the entire Oldston district police force — family! He'd effectively swapped one of Manchester's most notorious villains for one of the force's highest ranking police officers. Could his life get any more bizarre?

"We must have a chat about that other business. The thing with your cousin, I mean. I'm sure we can stop it going too far and quash any gossip before it takes root."

"I'd like to know how the gossip got started, sir, never mind trying to stop it."

"Someone had a word in my ear, Tom. That's all I can say for the time being."

Whoever that was, they were a slimy bastard. So, the chief super would try to sort it out. That was nepotism for you. No one had been keen to sort anything when the DCI had spoken to him earlier.

Sam caught hold of his arm. "Come and meet my son, Callum." Calladine was only too pleased to get away. With an apologetic smile at the chief . . . his uncle, he went with her gladly.

"He's one of my big bosses."

"Yes, I know; you were squirming big style back there. But don't worry. He does what Ma tells him."

"Calladine! What are you doing here?"

The sound of that voice made him wince. He turned round and there she was. Rhona Birch. She'd done her best, but her black dress was far too tight and she bulged everywhere. She must have decided against heels and her flatties did nothing for the overall look.

"I'm a guest, like you."

"I'll go and find Callum." Sam moved away.

"I wouldn't have thought this was your sort of venue." The DCI wore a sour expression on her face.

"You'd be surprised, ma'am."

"I'm here with Edwin, the chief. I don't want to appear rude, but who invited you?"

"My mother." At that moment Amy joined him and linked her arm with his.

"So your mother knows Eve Buckley, does she?"

There was a few seconds silence, during which Calladine performed a mental dance of joy. It had been a hellish day, but it was about to get a whole lot better. He smiled slightly.

"My mother *is* Eve Buckley," he said, savouring the moment as the woman's haughty expression changed to one of utter disbelief.

He squeezed Amy's hand and ushered her towards Sam, who was standing in the hallway with a teenage boy. He whispered in Amy's ear. "What's she doing now?"

"I don't think she's capable of doing much yet. She's still picking her jaw up off the floor."

Chapter 8

Next day, Rocco was at the nick before him — as usual. "More bones have turned up, guv. Miriam Gallimore rang in; they were delivered this morning in the post. I've told her not to touch them and we'll be round as soon as we can."

Calladine scanned the list of helpers at the homeless village. The Gallimores were on it, Miriam and Colin. "The bones are a bit of a puzzle. At least they're not human. I suppose we should be thankful for that, but I don't see the point."

"Scare tactics; someone trying to frighten the helpers. If that's the case then we should ask who would benefit from getting rid of the camp."

"Damien Chase is the obvious candidate. The blood is the real worry though. Where's the rest of whoever it belonged to?" Calladine went to the incident board, hands in trouser pockets, and stared at it for a few moments. "I don't think the two things are connected."

"Why not, sir?"

"I can't give you any reason, Rocco. It's just a gut feeling."

Ruth joined them, looking annoyed. "Damn traffic! Some sort of flood on the High Street. The water people have got the road up and everything. What with that and the tented village growing bigger every day, Leesdon is fast becoming a no-go area."

"What about Cerys? Isn't she sorting stuff out down there?"

"I drove past. But even if she was there I don't see what she could do about it. Yesterday there was about two dozen. I bet there's at least another ten this morning."

"Word gets round," said Rocco. "They've got food, shelter and medical treatment if they want it. It's a safer bet than dossing down on a park bench."

"The Gallimores — are they at home?" asked Calladine.

"Waiting for us to call, sir," said Rocco.

"Okay, take a uniform with you, collect the package and drop it off at the Duggan."

"More bones?" Ruth asked.

"Yep. And I still don't know what they mean."

"Anything on the missing man?"

"No. Still missing, and nothing's come in overnight."

Imogen looked up from her computer screen. "I've trawled through the records, guv. There's no 'Snap' but plenty of Langtons listed."

"Dead end, then?"

"Well, not entirely. I had a look at social media too. A man called Stuart 'Snap' Langton has a Facebook account. It's not up to date; there's been nothing posted for the last six months, which would fit. But he did have a number of 'friends,' and some of them have the same surname."

"Family!"

"Looks like it. Come and see."

Calladine looked at a photo showing a young man standing with a small boy on a beach. He had dark hair and was smiling happily. He bore scant resemblance to the photo Cerys had given him, but when she'd taken it he'd already been living rough for some time. "Start contacting some of those people. See what you can get. And good work."

"There is more — look at this." She showed him a page dedicated to Stuart Langton's business. He was a photographer, specialising in weddings. He had a large number of reviews, all of them good and there was also a sample of his work.

"That was where he got his nickname from, snapping pictures. If this is Snap, why give it all up to live rough?"

"I'll do some checking. It shouldn't take long," said Imogen. "Fancy another look round the village, Ruth?" Calladine wanted to know more about Snap Langton — and the rest of them too. He knew that many homeless people had substance abuse or mental health issues, but you couldn't presume anything.

"Okay. I'll just grab a coffee from the canteen. Meet you at the car."

"If you get anything that shows Snap is our man, let me know at once."

As he walked past the office, DI Brad Long called out. "Tom! What's your take on the Harrop case?"

"Got you chasing shadows, has she?" Calladine grinned.

"Too bloody right she has. The woman's got a screw loose," Brad replied.

"I think it was an inside job. You need to speak to the workforce."

"What do you base that on?"

"Not enough noise the night it happened. Rocco asked all along that street and the only thing folk heard was the heavy piece of plant used to break through the warehouse wall."

"Harrop himself, then?"

"Could be. If not, you can bet he'll be getting a cut and most of his stock back when everything goes quiet."

"Cut?"

"Insurance, Brad. In fact — start there. Find out how much and how long ago it was taken out."

"Thanks, Tom. I'll do that."

Poor Brad. God help us having to crack a case and put up with that woman at the same time, Calladine thought to himself.

* * *

Ruth sat down beside him in the car. "I've completely gone off tea. It should be the other way round; coffee is usually what mums-to-be can't stomach."

"Didn't get me one, then?"

"You didn't ask. But never mind that. How did you get on last night?"

He chuckled. "I rather enjoyed it. Eve was very welcoming and Sam was okay too."

"What's amused you?"

"The new DCI was there — Rhona Birch. She came on all high and mighty; asking what a pleb like me was doing at a function like that. You should have seen her face when I told her."

"She'll hate that. From what I've heard she likes to keep her people well and truly under her thumb. You being related to the posh end of Leesworth will bug her no end."

"Oh, and it gets better. Guess who my new uncle is?"

"Go on, surprise me."

"Chief Superintendent Edwin Walker, no less."

"You're joking!"

"No — he's Eve's brother. Rhona Birch will really hate me for that."

"Can't do your career any harm though, can it? It's about time you had a break on that front. Edwin Walker is rumoured to be a pretty fair sort of bloke."

"Time will tell, but I bet he's not best pleased to have me in the clan."

He drove them through the town, turning into the High Street. Half way along, it was closed to traffic.

"It's flooded — I did tell you. We could get to Chase Mill by the back way."

"What's it all about?"

"No idea. Perhaps it was all that rain last night. I'm surprised you didn't hear it."

"I was dead to the world — all that lovely scotch at the party."

All around Leesdon the traffic was crawling, bumper to bumper. When they eventually pulled into the grounds of Chase Mill, Ruth whistled. "There are more than ever now! There's at least another dozen or so since yesterday. I know they all have problems, but this can't continue, surely?"

"It looks like someone agrees with you." Calladine nodded at a middle-aged man strutting around with a clipboard. "What d'you think? Council?"

"Let's go have a word with Cerys."

"Your colleague has taken the bones," said Cerys, when they had caught up with her.

"They're not human, remember. I've no idea why they were sent but we'll get there," Ruth said.

"Well, it's got us all twitchy and no mistake, including the folk who live here."

"About that — is there no limit on the numbers you can take?"

She nodded towards the man with the clipboard. "No one's ever said anything, but *he* might once he's finished bawling at people. He arrived this morning from the council. They've not really bothered before, so I don't know what's happened. People come and go; it usually evens itself out."

"Why is this place so crowded? Don't they have anywhere else to go?" Calladine asked.

Cerys shook her head. "Obviously not. It's hard out there. Lose your job, can't pay the rent, the bills mount up and no one wants to know. If you've no safety net, no family, no network of friends, then that's it."

Calladine suddenly felt foolish for asking.

"You must know what sort of a world we're living in, Inspector? You do know about the unemployment, and the hardship? They throw you off benefits for any little thing, these days."

"It can happen to any of us," said Ruth.

Calladine knew about Leesdon's poverty alright, but it had never before spilled onto the streets like this. Something had gone terribly wrong. "Tell me about Snap. Why was he here?"

"Like your sergeant and I are trying to explain — hard times. I don't pry. Some tell me things, and some don't. Snap was running a business, and it failed. He couldn't get a job so he couldn't pay the mortgage on his flat. One thing led to another: the bank foreclosed, he couldn't get any help and he became clinically depressed. He finally had enough of dossing down on other people's sofas and took off. He had a difficult few months on the streets and then he came here. Snap had been roughed up several times. I found him in A & E when I went there with another bloke. I brought him back with me."

"Did he say what that business was?"

"We think he was a photographer. That's where the name came from."

"Did you ever see him with a camera? Did he ever say anything about taking photos?"

"Not that I'm aware of. He never showed anyone. But if he did have a camera, he'd have kept it quiet. Things do get stolen here, Inspector. These people are desperate. Despite the help we give them, a lot are on drugs. Money is hard to come by."

"We're going to have to search his tent and go through his things."

"Try and be discreet. I don't want to scare the others away. I'll have an initial look, get his stuff and keep it safe."

"Okay. I'll send someone back later."

Ruth nudged him. "What d'you reckon is going on over there?"

"What are you looking at?"

"Those two women. They look troubled, as if they're looking for someone."

"It happens all the time," said Cerys. "People come here hoping to find a loved one or a friend that's missing. I guess you could say we collect people."

"I'm going to have a word."

Ruth walked towards them.

* * *

The two women were walking from tent to tent. The older of the two was showing a photo to everyone she met. The other one followed, shaking her head.

Ruth approached them. "Hello! I'm from Leesdon CID. Me and my colleague are here investigating a case. I couldn't help but notice that you're doing a little investigating of your own. Can I ask what about?"

"We're not doing anything wrong. Just looking for someone, that's all."

"Me and my mum are looking for my sister," said the younger woman. "See. This is her." She showed Ruth a photo of a young woman with long blonde hair. She was smiling, and there was a slightly wistful look on her pretty face. "Lauren Steele. She's been missing for nearly three months."

"Have you reported it?"

"Of course, but the police weren't much help. I have to say that surprised me: Lauren is only seventeen."

"What did they do?"

"They came round, spoke to us both and took some of her stuff away. They spoke to her friends at college, asked a lot of questions. There was a piece in the local paper and on the news. After a while Mum was asked to give a DNA sample. That was scary. We didn't know if they'd found something awful."

"And nothing happened on the back of that?"

"No. After a couple of weeks they brought her laptop back and said they'd found nothing on it that helped."

"She texted me," said the mother. "Lauren said she was fine and we weren't to worry. But that's a big ask, isn't it? When you've no idea where she is or what she's doing."

The woman looked tired and drawn. This had obviously hit her hard. "Which station did you report it to?"

"Oldston. That's where we live. I wouldn't have come here, but I just have to do something. I can't stand much more of sitting about waiting for Lauren to turn up. It's been so long and it's tough. I get this awful feeling that something dreadful has happened to her."

"Lauren doesn't do this sort of thing," said her sister. "She's a quiet girl. She goes to the sixth-form college and wants to be a nurse. Does that sound like someone who'd run away?" The woman began to cry and her daughter put her arm round her shoulder.

"When I get back to Leesdon station I'll find out where they've got to. If they've found anything, I'll let you know. Here's my card. Ring me tomorrow and I'll give you an update."

"Thanks."

Ruth went back to join Calladine. "They're looking for a missing girl. It was reported to Oldston weeks ago but they got nowhere. They're both really cut up, particularly the mother."

"Naturally."

"Apparently the girl had a settled life; she was going to college and had ambitions for the future."

"Well, something must have been wrong if she ran away — a boy perhaps?"

"I'll check it out. They must get a lot of that here, folk looking for the missing. It's sad — a teenager takes off, leaves no word except one text and the family is just left dangling. Why can't we do more?"

"Because we can't always find them, that's why. Nine times out of ten there's a boyfriend involved or an argument in the family. They take off and end up in the city: Manchester or even London. We have limited resources. We don't know anything about this case. My advice is to leave it to Oldston for the time being."

"She said her daughter was quiet, studious, not the type to do something like this."

"They never are."

"I'm going to mingle."

"This isn't some kind of party, you know."

A queue had formed by the food counter. Cerys Powell was dishing up lunch. Ruth stood back and watched for a few minutes.

Cerys called to her. "Ron's gone missing. The bloke I was at the medical centre with, the one with the bad leg."

A man interrupted her. "Cut the chat and dish the grub out."

"If you don't calm down, Newt, you'll go to the back of the queue."

Ruth watched as he slammed the plate down and strode off.

"He's very volatile, that one. Got a temper, and he's handy with his fists too."

"Who is he?"

"Newt. That's what we call him. His surname is Newton, I think."

Ruth wrote it down in her notebook. "Could Ron have moved on?"

"No, he wouldn't do that. I've got his medication and everything. If he'd wanted to leave, he would have told me."

Ruth could see that she was worried. "Where does he go, during the day, I mean?"

"His usual spot is outside the library. I know the law doesn't want them begging but most days he sits there with the dog." Cerys nodded towards a skinny mongrel, hanging around at the edge of the lunch queue. "The dog is lost without him."

"He's not there today? Has anyone checked?"

"Eddie went out to look for him earlier, but there was no sign of him."

She handed over to Drusilla Patten and came round to stand beside Ruth.

"Look — he's in some sort of trouble, he's got to be. Ron is a creature of habit. He was one of the first here. He likes routine and he likes a base he can rely on. We've given him that. He wouldn't leave willingly. That's what I keep worrying about."

"I'll tell uniform when I get back to the station. They'll keep an eye out for him."

Cerys thrust his file at her. "He still has the bad leg. He's taken hardly any of those pills the doc gave him. There hasn't been time."

"I'll let you know as soon as we've got something. Try not to worry. He might have met someone, an old friend." But Ruth could see that Cerys wasn't convinced. She walked back to where Calladine was standing.

* * *

"We've got to go. We've got another one. A rag soaked in blood has been found in a skip on Co-op Street, just round the corner."

"In a skip? Are we sure some builder didn't have an accident?"

"It's a lot of blood, and it was the builder who reported it. The skip is there because of alterations to a shop front. He was dumping rubble this morning and saw it there."

"Cerys has another one missing. That man, Ron, the one I saw her with at the medical centre yesterday, the one with the bad leg. I have her notes on him here."

"I've told Julian. I want his people to have a good look at that street, see if there's anything else."

"We had a lot of rain last night, remember? If there was anything on the road or pavement it could well have been washed away."

The area was cordoned off, with a uniformed officer standing guard.

"The bloke who found it?" asked Calladine.

The uniform pointed to the shop.

The two detectives went inside, where the builder was having a mug of tea. "I thought it was some sort of prank. But it must have been quite a fight to leave a mess like that."

"Are there any cameras here?"

"No, there's nothing down here. Most of them are on the High Street."

Ruth was peering through the window. "There aren't any houses around here either, sir. It's all shops or offices with empty rooms upstairs."

"Whoever this bastard is, he knows what he's doing. He chooses his sites well. He must have a good knowledge of Leesdon, side streets and all."

"Even so, the High Street is only yards away and there's a pub at the end. He was taking a risk."

Calladine went outside and walked round the skip. There was nothing on the ground to suggest anything had happened here but, as Ruth had said, it had rained heavily. He walked a short distance along the street. "Where does this lead to?"

"Turn left and you're heading towards the Hobfield. Turn right and right again, and it's the mill.

"There's a dead end!"

"No there isn't. At the end of the street is that track they all use."

Calladine checked his watch. They still hadn't checked out that track. It would take Julian at least fifteen minutes to get here from the Duggan. "Let's go for a little walk."

At the top of the street they turned into a narrower one, and at the end was the track. On the left Calladine could see the tower blocks of the estate in the distance. The track was narrow, long, and appeared to lead round to the back of the mill.

"If you didn't know about it, you'd never know this path was here."

"It's a short cut. Folk will have used it to save having to walk all the way round."

"There's a lot of rubbish lying around. Be careful, Ruth."

Despite the number of people currently living in the camp, the narrow track didn't look as if it was used much. It had been tarred at one time, but it was worn away and after the storm the holes were filled with water. There was a tall wire fence on one side and an old stone wall on the other. Grass and weeds at the edges were littered with broken bottles and other rubbish.

"It's quiet and the ground's very rough. I'm surprised they venture along here in the dark."

"Not unless they know exactly what they're doing. You can see how it bends round. I reckon it comes out somewhere at the back of the mill."

"I think we'll get CSI to take a look. See what they come up with."

Chapter 9

But it wasn't Julian Batho who greeted them. Instead, Rhona Birch stood waiting for them, hands on her hips.

"Why is one of my DIs running around checking skips? I'd have thought you had plenty to do, Inspector, without inventing work. What have you got — a rag with a drop of blood on it? Keep this up Calladine and, uncle or no uncle, I'll have your badge."

Her small, dark eyes were full of venom. Damn the woman. He couldn't work like this. But what could he tell her? This wasn't officially a crime scene, not like Dale Lane, and he could hardly start talking about his instincts twitching. "We should wait for forensics, ma'am, before jumping to conclusions. We had something similar yesterday. A blood-soaked coat. Forensics confirmed that it was in fact a crime scene. Plus there are two men missing from the camp over there."

"It's more likely that when the pubs turned out last night that there was a fight and someone got a bloody nose. This isn't what we pay you for."

She was enjoying this. Was it payback for yesterday evening? She must have been royally pissed off when she learned who his new uncle was.

A van pulled up, disgorging two people wearing white coveralls.

Rhona Birch tapped her foot. "More cost. Complete waste of time."

Calladine ignored her. "The bloodied rag was found in the skip but I don't think the deed was done here. I'd like you to take a look at the trail at the end of the road. DS Bayliss will show you."

"Inspector, currently we have an issue with cost control. The facilities at the Duggan are excellent but they are pricey."

"I want the rag tested, and they might just get something from a track up there. This is a route taken by people walking to and from the camp."

"Those people don't settle; they come and go with no word. You know that."

"Not the two who are missing. One of them is ill and he left without his medication."

"So what now?" Birch asked.

"I'll get the blood matched against another sample."

Calladine turned his back on her and phoned Doc Hoyle. "You know the bloke you saw the other day? The one called Ron, who came in with Cerys Powell from the homeless village."

"Yes, I remember him."

"Did you take a blood sample for any reason, Doc?"

"I did actually, Tom. It does no harm to do a full blood count every now and again."

"Could a sample of his blood be sent over to the Duggan? Julian can check it against something we've found today. He's missing. Cerys Powell is concerned, and we've found something."

"She'll be upset if anything has happened to him. Cerys is very protective about her people. I'll sort that for you right away."

"Thanks, Doc. See you Saturday."

Moments later, Calladine's mobile rang again. It was Amy.

"Can we meet later at mine? It's my friend, Faye — she really needs to talk to you. Will you come round? Say about eight."

"What's she done? Do I bring the cavalry?"

"No, you bring a sympathetic ear and promise some positive help. Something more than the police are currently giving her."

"Faye who? Do I know her?"

"Faye Steele, and no you don't. No reason why you should. She's done nothing wrong."

She sounded annoyed. Calladine pulled a face as she rang off. He pocketed his mobile and turned to face Birch. "The blood on the rag will be tested against a sample that's being sent to the Duggan as we speak. If it checks out, then we will have to investigate further, ma'am. Costs or no costs."

"Well, I think you're wasting police time, and it's not good enough. I'm disappointed, DI Calladine. You are a maverick and that isn't what today's force needs or wants. My advice is; change tactics before it's too late. Having an uncle in an elevated position will not be much help once the proverbial hits the fan."

She got back into her car and drove off.

So it *was* about the night before!

Ruth caught the tail end of the conversation. "That's you told."

"For a while there, I was afraid she was going to hang around."

"She does have a point in a way. We don't have anything concrete."

"We have two missing men, one crime scene and now this. Sooner or later the bodies will surface, Ruth. Mark my words."

* * *

And that was what he told the rest of the team when they got back to the nick. "We're waiting on results from the Duggan. With a bit of luck we might get a positive ID. But if I had to speculate, I'd say the first crime scene involved Stuart Langton, otherwise known as 'Snap.'"

"He may not have been the victim, sir. The blood could belong to someone else. Someone he had a fight with. It went too far and now he's done a runner," said Rocco.

He had a point. Calladine looked at the young detective for a moment and then wrote the word 'victim' on the board, followed by a question mark. "The coat in the bin had Langton's ring in the pocket. Even if he did start something, I doubt he'd have left that behind."

"It could have been stolen from him," said Imogen. "It was his ring. I rang some of the people he was friends with on Facebook. One of them is his sister. She confirmed that he's been missing for about six months. He had a girlfriend he sometimes stayed with, who lived somewhere in Cheshire. Apparently Snap wasn't keen on sharing any details about his private life with his family, so she couldn't tell me anything else."

"Well done! But whatever happened, a lot of blood was spilt. It looks like whoever did the attacking tried to clean up afterwards. The latest find looks similar, and another inhabitant of the village is missing — one Ron Weatherby."

"Do we have a motive for any of this, sir?" asked Rocco.

"Nothing obvious. We need to speak to everyone who helps out in the village. We need to find out if Snap and Ron knew each other."

"They did, sir. They even shared a tent if you recall. Cerys told us," said Ruth.

"Was that something that happened because they arrived together, knew each other before, or was it just a random arrangement? We need to know."

"Do you think this is linked to the bones?" said Imogen.

"I didn't, but now I'm not so sure. The two things are very different. The bones were carefully wrapped and sent to named individuals. The clothing we've found is different. Given that no one has taken themselves to the hospital, plus the volume of blood lost, there must be at least one body out there somewhere."

"They won't stay hidden forever," said Ruth.

"They might, if they've been buried," said Rocco.

"I want a presence in that camp — day and night. I want the place watching, but without making it obvious. We need to know exactly who's living there and when they finally leave for good."

"They will resent that, sir," Ruth said.

"Tell them you're investigating Snap's disappearance, but no more. It's for their protection. Someone out there is killing homeless men and until we catch the bastard it's in their interests to play ball with us."

"Cerys will help; they listen to her. We need to do all we can to get her on board. She said that most nights they had kids from the Hobfield bothering them. We can use that as our reason for posting a uniform there."

"Good idea, but they must be undercover. I don't want any panic. If we are too heavy-handed they'll scarper, and one of them might be the killer. For now we keep the possible victims' identities to ourselves."

"You will not put anyone in there, undercover or otherwise!" Rhona Birch stood at the doorway. "It would not be cost effective, Inspector. So don't do it — understand?" She turned and walked back to her office.

Before Calladine could say anything, Imogen waved from her desk.

"Sir, I've found out a bit more about Snap. His sister was right. He did have a regular girlfriend; the boy in the photo is her son, not his. Apparently his business failed big style and he couldn't cope. They argued a lot. She got him to the doctors and he was put on anti-depressants, then he overdosed and ended up in hospital. He recovered, discharged himself and she hasn't seen him since. All this information comes from his mother. She's just replied to an email I sent her."

"Did anyone report him missing?"

"Yes, his mother did, and that was roughly nine months ago. She also says that she has received one letter from him, postmarked Leesdon."

Calladine wrote the word 'letter' next to Snap's name on the board.

"He didn't say much, just that he was okay and that he'd write again. A few lines, she says, that was all."

"Thanks, Imogen, good work. Would you see what you can get on Ron Weatherby now? He appears to have needed medical treatment on numerous occasions, but he's travelled a lot. See what you can do."

Joyce was holding out the office phone for him. "Call for you, sir."

"Is that you, Tom?"

His face creased into a frown. He recognised the voice — just, but she wouldn't ring him here, surely?

"Marilyn? Is that you?"

"Yes, Tom. I need to speak to you. In person would be better. Can we meet?"

Marilyn was Ray Fallon's wife. She had stood by Ray over many years, regardless of the heinous crimes he committed.

"Not really. It wouldn't be on. I'm due in court very soon to testify against him — you know that. You shouldn't be speaking to me at all.

"You don't understand, Tom. I have to see you. I have to tell you . . . warn you. Ray is off his head. He's been saying all kinds of things, threatening. I'm worried he'll do something stupid."

"Warn me about what? Regardless of what he threatens, that bastard can't do much from where he is.

Last time I looked, Strangeways seemed reasonably secure to me."

"You don't know him like I do. You haven't had to listen to the things he's been saying. He didn't like you before, but since you got the evidence to nail him, he hates you with a passion. He's obsessed. Really."

"Stop worrying, Marilyn. If he bothers you, don't visit so often. The man's a menace, he always has been. He's locked up good and tight, Marilyn. He had no way of getting in touch with his people on the outside. The prison authorities will have seen to that." Well, he hoped they had.

"Ray can get round all that — he's done it before. He greases palms and people do his bidding. Please be careful, Tom."

The line went dead. Calladine shook his head. Could there be anything in that? Something had her spooked. Surely the prison would ensure that Fallon was kept tight. But if that was the case, why was Marilyn so worried? He hadn't spoken to her in years. After what the DCI had said and now her phone call, he just wanted the whole crazy business with his cousin over.

Calladine saw Ruth yawning and rubbing her belly. She'd been standing at the back of the office and now sat down at her desk.

"Take off if you want. We need the positive IDs before we can really get going."

"Okay — see you all tomorrow. Don't go doing anything stupid about Birch. Let it lie for now."

"Now it's Birch and Fallon's wife, Marilyn. That was her on the phone."

"Wants you to get him off, does she?"

"No she wants to warn me. Apparently the idiot's been making threats."

"In that case do as she says and take care." She tapped his arm. "Let's just hope that her ringing you here isn't seen as you colluding with the enemy," she whispered.

"This is doing my head in. I need to get some work done. Rocco, you and I will go talk to the other helpers. But first we'll pay a visit to Damien Chase. After all, it is his mill."

"I'll ring him, sir, and tell him we're on our way."

* * *

Damien Chase was descended from a Victorian cotton baron. At one time Chase Mill would have employed most of the local population — including some of his own ancestors, Calladine thought. The town had a lot to be grateful to that family for, but all that was in the past. The cotton industry was long gone and nothing had replaced it. Chase Mill lay empty and crumbling. As the detective looked at the huge stone house he wondered how much of that old money remained. Looking after a place like this would cost a fortune. Joyce had done some basic research and Chase didn't have a huge income. He was registered as the owner of three clubs in the area and, according to the latest filed accounts, they weren't doing very well.

"Welcome, Inspector!" Damien Chase greeted them with a smile, and led them inside. "My lawyer rang me this morning. Cerys Powell should be one worried girl. She's bright. I'm surprised she's still intent on playing the do-gooder."

"You don't approve, I take it." Calladine and Rocco followed him into the sitting room.

"No I bloody well don't! That lot are costing me a fortune. I've got a buyer ready to go, but they want the homeless people out. My lawyer will serve them final notice tomorrow, so if they don't pack up and move on, I can finally send in the bailiffs and have them forcibly removed."

"You'd do that?"

"Too true I would. That land is valuable and I need the money."

"Have you done anything else to encourage them to leave, Mr Chase?"

"What do you take me for, Inspector? Eager to be rid of them, I might be, but I'm not stupid. Everything I do is strictly within the law, expensive as that is."

"There will be a lot of disappointed people."

"Not my problem — nor is it yours."

"It might not be that simple. We are currently investigating the disappearance of two men from the camp."

Chase shrugged. "I don't see what that has to do with me. These people live on the margins of society, and according to their own rules. So you can't lay that one at my door."

Chase was younger than Calladine had expected. He was tall and slim, with dark hair. He had no wife, no kids and, as far as Calladine knew, lived in this sprawling house alone.

"You do want them off your land though?"

"I certainly do and the sooner the better. They moved in, set things up and then got the council to provide the showers and so on. I wasn't even consulted. Damned cheek, if you ask me. But they won't get away with it. If I lose this deal, or have to renegotiate on the price, then I'll sue."

"What are the plans for the land?"

"Chase Mill is a prime site. A small housing estate and a row of shops."

"Do you have any other business interests?"

"Yes. I own three clubs, one in Oldston and two in Manchester. They do good trade but I have heavy overheads. I have the upkeep of this place and the mill. Frankly, Inspector, I need every penny I can get."

"Don't you have a social conscience, Mr Chase?" Rocco asked.

"Not in this case. It's costing me a packet every day it remains unsold. I pay a security company to keep an eye on the place. If one of those people has an accident, I could be sued. The mill building is dangerous. I tell them, I instruct security to keep them out, I've had signs put up but still they wander all over the place. Sometimes they even sleep in there, I know. Plus the devils off that estate have stripped the lead off the roof and helped themselves to dozens of the roofing tiles. I need to sell and quick. Chase Mill is a court case waiting to happen."

"I'd like to speak to your security people if I may. Who are they? Do they watch over the place at night?"

"They're called 'Ace Security.' Supposedly they're there at night. I pay a fee that covers twenty-four hours."

"If they have camera footage it might be useful," said Rocco.

"They will have. I'll have a word and get them to hand it over."

"Where are the cameras placed, sir?"

"Not everywhere, I'm afraid. There's one inside — the ground floor — and another along the roof."

"Have you received any packages containing bones, Mr Chase?" Calladine asked.

"No. I heard about that. Wish I'd thought of it first. If you want my opinion, it looks as if there's more than just me wants them out."

"Thank you, Mr Chase. You've been very helpful."

"Nice enough bloke," said Rocco, as they returned to the car. "He must rattle around in that huge house, though. If money's that tight you'd think he'd sell and buy something smaller."

"Not our concern, Rocco. What's more important is that he does seem set on selling. As far as I can see, he's the only one who'll gain by getting rid of the camp. So for now, regardless of what he says or how he comes across, that fact keeps him in the frame."

Chapter 10

The candle had almost burned away to nothing. If he didn't come back soon, she'd be in total darkness. Mirela hammered on the window once again, but it was hopeless. It was boarded up both inside and out. During the daylight hours a faint glimmer shone through along one side. But there was no chance of making an escape that way.

She started to sob. There was no furniture so she hunkered down in a corner of the room. The clothes he'd given her to wear were not suitable for the cold. He'd dressed her in an ultra-short dress with a skimpy top and had forbidden her to wear underwear. He wanted her to look like a slut. It was what the customers expected. When she complained, he beat her. Faded bruises marred the pale, normally flawless skin of her arms and upper body.

Mirela didn't know what time it was or even what day. He said it was only a few weeks since he'd brought her here from Bucharest, but it seemed like a lifetime ago. As each day passed she doubted she'd ever return. He would never let her go. She — or rather her body — was too popular with the men. The thought of never seeing her mother or her home village again made her cry harder. This wasn't how it was supposed to be.

He'd been one of Anna's friends on Facebook and when she'd gone missing, Mirela had asked his advice. He'd seemed concerned and offered to help. After they'd communicated for a few weeks he said he liked her. He wanted her to come to the UK so they could search for her sister together. He promised her a good life and once they found Anna, they'd both want for nothing.

He'd been clever, moving slowly and winning her trust. He'd told her he knew where Anna was. He tempted her with the lure of well-paid work for her and her sister. He'd said she'd be able to send money home, bring her family here for a holiday. What a joke. She'd been a complete fool. But he'd been so charming. To begin with he was nice, friendly. He appeared to show genuine concern when her mother was taken ill. Mirela needed money to pay for her treatment, and he'd helped. He'd said she could pay him back from her wages once she came to the UK. Now she owed him, and every day the debt grew because of the interest he added.

Her family suspected nothing. If they ever found out the truth she'd die of shame. He'd allowed her to ring her mother just once and had told her what to say. She was to laugh and tell her that all was well. She was to talk about the good job she'd found and say she was earning lots of money. They must never know the truth. If they found out, she could never go back.

* * *

"Mirela! What are you doing, girl?"

A pool of light illuminated the tiny room as the door opened. He cursed as she buried her face in her hands. She was hard work. He had no time for women who were scared of their own shadows.

"Mac! Is that you?"

"Who the fuck d'you think it is? Get up. Fix your hair and come along with me." He tossed her a brush and watched as she dragged it through her long, black hair.

"Stand up and smile. A happy face makes the punters happy. Then they'll pay more." He stepped forward and pinched both her cheeks. "You need some colour. You look like a bloody ghost."

"I'm hungry and cold. You leave me in this place all day. What do you expect?"

"I don't expect backchat for starters. We have a deal, remember? You need to earn the money you owe me. You do understand that, don't you Mirela?"

She spat back at him in broken English. "I owe you nothing! You are a pig! You trick me. I should be looking for my sister not being kept prisoner by you." She was standing now, her small fists clenched as he walked towards her.

He took hold of her arm and whacked her hard across the side of the head with the flat of his hand. "I'm used to dealing with the likes of you, bitch. Cross me again and I'll sort you for good. Anna's long gone, so don't waste your time worrying about her."

"Was she here? Did you see her?"

"Yes she was here. She was even more useless than you are, so I dealt with her. End of."

Mirela was shaking, he could see, and it turned him on. She was small and thin and he loved the power he had over her. She must be taught a lesson. Later, after she'd serviced tonight's clients, he'd give her some real grief. She needed to learn who was boss. Then she wouldn't be so keen to answer back.

"Don't hurt me, Mac. Please don't hit me again!"

His mobile was ringing. He shoved the girl into the corner of the room and answered it.

"You should watch your step," said the voice. "You're attracting too much attention, Mac. You're in danger of becoming a liability."

"Don't give me that. You know nothing. It's me that takes all the risks. Anyway, the pigs are chasing their tails. They know nothing."

"We don't want them finding out the truth, do we? We need them to stop sniffing around the camp. It's too close for comfort."

"They can go where they want. They're looking for missing men; nothing to do with our little operation."

"Just look after your end and don't draw attention to yourself. Get us into bother and I'll have your hide. You always were a loser. Can't think straight under pressure, never could. I've got work to do, money to earn, and the last thing I want is you cracking at the first sign of trouble. If the police do come poking their noses in, you must make sure they get it all wrong. They must find nothing. Alright." The caller hung up.

Mac looked at Mirela and shook his head. She was a time bomb. She might be pretty and popular but she couldn't stay here. He'd do a trade; get a fresh face, but not tonight. Right now there was money to be made out of that perfect little body. "Get ready and do as you're told. I've got a punter waiting. Cross me, answer back one more time and I'll kill you. Understand?"

* * *

It had been a long and troubling day with nothing to show for it. Calladine decided he'd drop in at Amy's on his way home and make arrangements for later. He turned into her street and parked outside her shop. He was looking forward to sitting beside her comfortable fire for a few minutes with a stiff drink in his hands. The wind was blowing and it was still raining. Then something caught his eye.

Fixed to the wall of Amy's shop there was a 'for sale' board.

He rubbed his eyes. Had he got the right shop? It had to be the property next door. But it wasn't. What was she playing at? If she was selling up, where the hell was she going? He was about to go in when his mobile rang. It was Rocco.

"You're needed, sir, on the High Street, where the roadworks are. A body has turned up. The workmen found it about thirty minutes ago."

Amy would have to wait until later. It was pointless taking his car; there was nowhere to park anyway. A walk in the night air would help clear his head.

The area was lit up and had been taped off. Calladine expected that the body would turn out to be Snap, or Ron. But it wasn't. As he walked over, a woman stepped forward.

"Natasha Barrington, Home Office Pathologist from the Duggan," she said.

"So you got the doc's job?"

"I suppose I did. But I'm not alone; there are three pathologists working at the Duggan. I do tend to get the Oldston and Leesworth cases, though."

"Settling in?"

"It's less hectic than I'm used to. I was at the Met. Now that was busy. Hardly had time to draw breath some days."

A coverall shrouded her from head to foot, so Calladine couldn't tell what she looked like.

"Given the weather, I'd say the body has been washed along the sewer by the flood water, but from where is anyone's guess."

"Male?"

She pushed down the hood of her white coverall and smiled at him. "Put this on and go take a look."

Calladine shrugged himself into the coverall she held out to him. He walked towards the hole in the road and ducked into the tent that covered it. To one side lay an old sack. It held an arrangement of bones — a human skeleton barely strung together.

Natasha stuck her head through the tent flap. "From the size of the femur and the pelvis I'd say female. I'll know for sure when I get that little lot back to the lab —

including whether you're looking at murder or something else."

Female. He hadn't expected that. This was turning out to be the week from hell. "How long has it been down there?"

She shrugged. "Can't say. The sack is hessian. Today I think they're more commonly made of polypropylene, which is more environmentally friendly, so being hessian might help or it might not. As for the bones . . ." Another shrug.

Now Calladine had yet another mystery to add to all the others. He counted them off in his head. Since the start of the week there'd been two heavily bloodied rags, someone sending bits of animal bone to the helpers at the camp and now a sack with a skeleton in it. And he didn't have a lead on any of it.

"You look done in. Fancy a drink? There's a pub over there."

She was pointing to the Wheatsheaf.

"Yes, why not? A quick one won't hurt. But I want this area treating as a crime scene until we know better."

"Whoever that was, they weren't killed here. The sack has been washed along the sewers, possibly for miles. And if it hadn't been in a sack, the skeleton would have broken up. The bones would have ended up all over the place and we'd have got nothing."

They watched as the sack and skeleton were removed, placed in a van and driven off to the Duggan. A workman in a hi-vis jacket called out to them.

"Can I finish off?"

"There really won't be much left here, if that's what you're thinking. The body wasn't left there for you to find," said Natasha Barrington.

Calladine nodded at the man.

"Still want that drink?"

"Give me a minute. You go and get them in. I'll have a red wine. And what do I call you? Inspector is a little formal."

He smiled at her. "Tom. And you?"

"Natasha, or Tash, I don't mind which."

Suddenly there was a scream from the workman's tent.

Calladine darted forward and looked inside. The hole had filled up again. He saw an arm in the water.

Natasha began to cover up. "Here we go again. Any ideas, Tom?"

There were two missing men but there had been more blood around the dustbin than at the skip. So it could be Snap. "Might have. If that arm belongs to who I think it does, then there should be a scar above the wrist."

He stepped back and waited. Natasha Barrington carefully fished out the arm and laid it on a large evidence bag.

"Yes, here it is. The scar's about nine centimetres long and quite recent."

"Six months, according to what I've been told. Get forensics to do a DNA profile, will you? And check it against the blood on the coat we found."

"You think this belonged to one of your missing homeless men?"

"Yes, I do, and it's pretty gruesome. Now I'm wondering what happened to the rest of him — and the other missing man."

"I'll finish up here. You go and get those drinks in. After this little lot we could do with them." If the arm did belong to Snap, it fell into place, but the female skeleton? Where did that come from?

* * *

Tash Barrington joined Calladine at the bar. She'd tidied her hair and was wearing lipstick. He was flattered: she'd made an effort.

"This your local?"

"I suppose it is. I live just around the corner."

"Ah, a Leesdon boy. You must like it here. Haven't you ever wanted to get out, try somewhere else, if only for a leg up the ladder?"

"I can't say I have. There are reasons why I've stayed a DI and they're a bit complicated. Nothing to do with not wanting to move, though. Besides, there's nothing wrong with Leesdon, you know."

"Depends on your point of view. From where I stand, Leesdon and Oldston keep my workload good and heavy. It's a hard place."

"You're not local, are you? It's the accent — I'm trying to place it."

"I'm not from far away. South Yorkshire — Chesterfield."

"Bring your family with you?"

"Now you're fishing, Tom. But I don't mind. Just so you know, I have one ex-husband and one son at boarding school. Neither of them gives me much trouble. You?"

"One ex-wife, who's now passed, and one daughter. She's the solicitor on the High Street, the one above the estate agents."

"Current love interest?"

"Now it's you who's fishing! If you'd asked me yesterday, the answer would have been a tentative yes. But now, I'm not sure. I've just had quite a shock. Seems my current love interest — as you put it — is selling up and moving on. In fact that's something I'm going to have to go and sort now." He looked at his watch.

"You're dumping me so soon?"

Her dark brown eyes were twinkling at him. He liked her, but he'd still have to go and talk to Amy, everything was happening too fast. He needed to find out what that damn sign was all about. Something told him she was about to drop a bombshell, and it wouldn't be pleasant.

"I have to sort something. The day hasn't ended on a very good note, has it? For either of us. This morning I had one mystery, but tonight I've got two bodies — well, one and an arm. Days like this wear me out. I wouldn't be good company anyway."

"In that case I'll let you off."

"We'll get together some other time. But for now I really do have to go, Natasha. Tash. I'll ring tomorrow." He bent and swiftly pecked her cheek.

What was he doing? The last thing he needed was the added complication of another woman in his life. Yet deep down, he knew that Amy wouldn't be bothered if he did have someone else. Where relationships were concerned, she didn't do ownership.

* * *

It was raining again. He'd be glad when today was done with. Outside Amy's door he looked up at the board. He'd not noticed before, but it was Jo's agency that was selling the place. So why hadn't she told him? Jo lived with his daughter Zoe, so she must know. He didn't have a key; Amy had never given him one, and so he banged on the door — hard.

"What's that all about?" he demanded, pointing upwards and then barging past her into the flat.

"I do keep asking you round but you can never make it. I would have told you sooner but it's not something I wanted to do on the phone."

"Why are you selling? You love this place. I don't understand."

"I want a change, Tom. It's time for me to move on."

"Move where, for God's sake?"

"I'm buying a place in Cornwall."

It took several seconds for this to sink in. "Cornwall! Why go there? What's wrong with this place? But more to the point, what about us?"

"I'm going there because it's where I want to live. I've made an offer on a cottage near St. Austell and it's been accepted."

"You've still not answered my question, Amy. What about you and me?"

"Tom, I've always been honest with you, right from the beginning. I was never looking for a serious relationship. I can't stay with one man for long; it's not how I am."

"So effectively it's over, that's what you're saying. You're buggering off and to hell with anything we might have."

"You've got some nerve. As I just said, I never gave you any indication that I was looking for someone permanent in my life. You're not being fair."

"Fair! I'm being sidelined for some bloody fantasy. Cornwall! Couldn't you get any further away from me?"

He turned to leave; she'd not even invited him upstairs. She didn't care, she never had. He'd simply been another one in a long line of many.

"My friend Faye came round. We waited but she had to go."

"Sorry. I had work to do."

"She needs your help, Tom. Her daughter's gone missing."

Calladine had had enough and he certainly didn't want to listen to this now. "I take it she's reported it to the police?"

"Yes, of course she has, but they've not been much help. Lauren has been gone for a couple of months. She's only seventeen and there's been no word."

He groaned. This, on top of everything else! But a skeleton of an unknown female had just been washed up out of a hole on the High Street.

"She's written everything down. Here." Amy thrust a file at him.

The name on it was 'Lauren Steele.'

Chapter 11

Thursday

"Ruth in yet?"

Imogen answered him from behind her computer screen. "She rang in sick. Apparently her blood pressure is sky-high, so she's on bed rest."

"Joyce, would you search out a report for me? It's a missing girl — made during the last three months or so. Her name is Lauren Steele. Her mother Faye will have reported it."

She gave an enthusiastic nod. He wished he could have a bit of whatever was motivating her.

"I'll do it right away. I'll leave a printout on your desk."

"No — email it to Ruth at home. She can do some research from her sofa. Won't do her any harm."

"Okay, sir. Will do."

"Right, Rocco, you're with me. We'll visit Ruth first, then the camp, before we go on to the Duggan.

"What are we doing about the skeleton, sir?" Imogen asked.

"I haven't decided yet. But you could look out a map of Leesdon's sewage system for me. It might help if we knew the direction of travel."

"Does that mean the sewers might have to be searched?" Imogen shuddered.

"It's a possibility. Depends how old the bones are."

"The report of the find is on the system, that's how I knew, and the case has been assigned to us."

Of course it had. Rhona Birch thought he needed something 'proper' to do. "I'm waiting for Doctor Barrington to give us an idea of the age before we dive in. Until we have something to go on, our priority is the arm. Anything else?"

The team exchanged looks.

"Er, DCI Birch was looking for you," Rocco said eventually.

"In that case let's get moving. You haven't seen me." Calladine sighed. "Birch isn't going to leave us alone, is she? Before we know it she'll be in the way, big style."

"There's always the possibility she won't stay. Imogen did some checking and in the last ten years she's been two years tops at all her posts," Rocco said.

"Perhaps she really is some sort of hatchet queen. We'll have to see."

* * *

Calladine and Rocco drove along the High Street.

"Traffic's cooled down since yesterday. I see the roadworks are still taped off," Rocco said.

"That's the water board. Doctor Barrington said the skeleton probably travelled in the water. The poor girl might not have met her end anywhere near here," replied Calladine.

They pulled up outside Ruth's house. Her and Jake's cars were both still on the drive. "At least she's got company."

Jake opened the door. "She's insisting she's okay, but that's not what the midwife said. Doesn't know when to call it a day, that's her problem. Come in!"

Ruth greeted them from the sofa. "He's not still going on, is he? Sorry about this, Tom, but I have to do as I'm told. I won't be back until my blood pressure is normal, I'm afraid."

So it was starting. The great expanse of time without her that Calladine had been dreading. "Just get well. Perhaps sticking it out at work isn't the best thing."

"Want rid of me, do you?"

"No! Far from it, as well you know. But while you're laid up, I did wonder if you were up to doing a little research . . ." He passed her Lauren Steele's file.

She smiled. "Yes, I think I could manage that. The people at the camp?"

"No, nothing to do with that. This is a missing teenage girl, one Lauren Steele. Her mother made the report a while ago, but she's never been found."

Ruth paged through the file, looking interested. "It was her mother and sister I met yesterday at the camp. Runaway kids; it should be taken more seriously but more often than not, it isn't."

"Lauren's mother gave Amy this file. Joyce will email you the official report. Have a look; see what you think. She could have a social media account, Facebook or something. See if she's posted anything recently."

"Apart from the Amy factor, why are you so concerned?"

"A skeleton was washed up out of those road works last night. All that rain we had must have dislodged the body from wherever it had been lying. Doctor Barrington thinks it's female. I know it's a long shot, but for some reason it's got me on edge and I can't dismiss it."

"I'll let you know the minute I have something. But you'll have to keep me up to date with what Doctor Barrington finds."

Calladine looked around. "Where's Jake gone?"

"I think he's showing Rocco his workshop." Ruth rolled her eyes.

"Natasha Barrington took me for a drink last night. I like her; she's nice."

"Well, that might be your opinion, but the grapevine says she's a man-eater. She even made a play for Greco at Oldston." Ruth giggled.

"Is she daft? How do you know that anyway?"

"Jed Quickenden told me. She got nowhere with Greco, so now she's set her cap at you. I'd be careful, the woman sounds desperate."

"Why desperate? Because she took me for a drink?"

"You're older than her and by quite a lick too. And what about Amy?"

"She's about to dump me."

"You must have got it wrong, surely?"

"No. She's selling up and moving to Cornwall — no discussion, no apologies, just bye-bye, Tom. I'm cut up about it but what can I do?"

"Oh, Tom. How do you do it? I am sorry — I know you're fond of her . . ."

"Jake's got a Mini Cooper in his workshop — an original!" Rocco was back, full of excitement.

Calladine was grateful. It stopped the conversation with Ruth getting too tricky, or maudlin.

"Don't get carried away. It's still in a right state, but I'll restore it eventually."

Ruth grinned at him. "Make the most of it, because you won't have time to draw breath once the baby comes. He's got no idea . . . Look — perhaps you've got it wrong about Amy. Talk to her again."

"Perhaps I will, but not yet. We've got a day full of stuff to get through first. I'll pop round or ring you later."

"They're a great couple, aren't they, boss?" said Rocco as they left.

Calladine nodded. Ruth had found her perfect partner in Jake Ireson.

* * *

Ruth was reading the file Calladine had left her. "I wonder why she left, where she went. You know more about teenage girls than I do — what are they into?" she asked Jake.

"Is that work?"

"Yep, but it's nothing heavy, just a little research."

"You're supposed to do nothing. No stress, the midwife said. Why not just watch TV and chill? Look at that stuff the birdwatching club sent you."

"If I start looking at that I'll just want to go on the trip and I can't, can I? In the meantime pass me the laptop and the phone, would you?"

"Where are they going?"

"Red kite chasing again, in Mid Wales. A woman there feeds them every day and apparently they wait for her. I hope the others get some good pictures. We're planning to put some on the calendar for next year. The one we do to raise money."

"You'll be able to join them again once the baby comes."

Ruth gave him a look. He obviously knew even less about babies than she did!

Jake placed laptop and phone gently across her knees. "As long as you're okay with it . . ."

"It's a little research, just the odd phone call. What harm can it do? Go on then — you were going to tell me about teenage girls. Come on, you must know a lot, you teach them every day."

"In my experience they giggle a lot, about everything. They like boys, make-up, playing around with their hair and they're constantly on their phones."

"So if one disappeared and didn't contact her friends or family, and didn't use her Facebook account, what would you say?"

"I'd say she dropped off the planet." Jake laughed, and made for the kitchen.

Ruth stared at the photo. "So where have you gone, Lauren?" she said to herself. The girl was pretty, with small features and a full mouth. Her blonde hair hung in a curtain, down to her shoulders. Lauren Steele was smiling, looking tanned and relaxed. Ruth tapped away for a few minutes, quickly finding the Facebook account. "There's no privacy set on this. Anyone who wants to can see everything she posts."

Jake returned with tea. "My lot live online. They post all the time, about nothing. Things of no interest to anyone usually, and often during class time."

"So did this girl, but not recently."

"In that case, I'd say it can only be because she can't."

"Don't say that, Jake. That sort of statement is heavy with possibilities."

"Well, I'm going to leave you to it. I'll have an hour on the mini if you don't mind, and then I'll do the shopping."

"Okay. I'll do you a list. We'll have lunch about midday — and you're making it."

Ruth needed more information. She'd have to speak to Lauren's mother.

"Mrs Steele? It's Sergeant Ruth Bayliss from Leesdon CID. We spoke briefly at the camp about your missing daughter. I work with Inspector Calladine, and the file you left with Amy Dean has been passed on to me. I'm looking at Lauren's Facebook account on my laptop as we speak. Did she have a computer of her own?"

"Yes, she has a laptop. It's in her room. The police had a look but brought it back the next day."

"In that case, could I have it? I'd like to look at her social media accounts, her emails; see who she was talking to before she disappeared."

"Oh that one's easy, I can tell you that. She'd become obsessed with some young man called Mac. They were messaging each other all the time."

"Could that be where she's gone? To be with him?"

"I don't know. If that was the case there's no reason why she wouldn't tell me. There's only me, Lauren and her sister. She's never been secretive about boyfriends before."

"Did you meet this Mac, Mrs Steele?"

"No. He was always working, so she said."

"Do you know his full name? Did Lauren ever call him anything but 'Mac?'"

"No, it was always just Mac. She'd known him about two months. Suddenly he seemed to be the only thing that mattered in her life. She stopped seeing her other friends and she even dropped out of school."

"Did she go to Leesdon Academy?"

"No, Oldston High. We live in Oldston, not Leesworth."

"Is that where you reported her missing, Oldston Station?"

"Yes, but they were very busy that night."

"Can I send someone round for the laptop? It'll be a uniformed officer. He'll issue a receipt and I'll make sure you get it back."

Mrs Steele began to cry. "All I want back is my Lauren. Find her, Sergeant, please — before it's too late."

"Too late? What else do you know, Mrs Steele?"

"Nothing. But I have a bad feeling. Lauren wouldn't do this to me. We're all very close: me, her and Lindsey. This is just not how she is."

"We'll do our best."

Ruth rang the nick and arranged to have the laptop picked up as soon as possible. She remained staring at the photo. The girl had a mother, a sister, a settled home and she attended school regularly. Someone had stepped in and tempted her away from all that. But who? This 'Mac' her mother had talked about? If so, how were they supposed to find him if that name was all they had to go on?

* * *

Calladine and Rocco pulled into Chase Mill and parked up. Calladine stood for a moment, looking at the huge red brick building. "There's supposed to be some sort of security here, that firm Damien Chase hired. Check it out will you, Rocco? See if they've got any CCTV footage. But be careful. Parts of the place are dangerous, I believe."

Calladine went up to the crowd around the food counter. There was some sort of argument going on.

"This is completely different! They were random; they weren't done up like the bones and targeted at certain people. Anyway, we have a far more serious problem to worry about now," Cerys shouted. She was waving a sheaf of official-looking papers.

"They're out to get us and it won't stop at them bones! You're forgetting about Snap and Ron," an irate elderly man replied.

"Hey! Calm down." Calladine could see that the man was getting increasingly riled and was having a good go at Cerys and Jean Patton.

"They were rats. These are bones. The rats were dead and left lying outside the tents every morning, just thrown around. This is nothing like that," Cerys said.

"And what's happened to Snap? Tell me that! If he'd taken off again, he would have told someone. This bloody place is cursed." The man spat on the ground and shuffled off.

"Charming," said Calladine.

"I can't blame him. Everyone is scared, Inspector. First Snap disappears and now Ron. They're all wondering who'll be next," Cerys said.

"Did they ever find out who was responsible for the rats?"

"No. I read in the paper that it was presumed to be locals trying to get rid of the camp. But no one wanted to know, and the council were no help at all."

He made a note of it nonetheless. The method might be different, but the perpetrators were probably after the same end result. "What have you got there?" He nodded at the paperwork.

"We've had the bailiffs round. At least I think that's who they were. Chase wants us out. He's got the law on his side so we don't have much choice. Whether we like it or not, we're going to have to pack up," Cerys said.

"How long have you got?"

"The letter says a week."

That wasn't long, and there wasn't much Calladine could do to help.

"If it's possible I'd like to trace Snap's movements on the day he went missing."

"He always followed the same routine. He used the shower block, queued here for breakfast and took it back to his tent to eat it. After that he usually had a chat with some of the others."

"Was he friendly with anyone in particular?"

"He got on with Ron. They shared a tent and looked out for one another. If they'd been out all day, they'd meet up and walk back together. Ron's leg had prevented that recently though, which was why he wasn't with him when — when whatever happened."

"How did they come to share? Did they already know each other?"

"No, but Ron's a quiet soul and Snap liked that. He was quite protective towards him."

"Okay, that's fine. We're going to have to search the tent they shared and take some things away. Is anyone else using it now?"

"Jack was, but he's moved in with someone else now, so no, it's empty."

"Keep it that way and don't let anyone in. I'll have a quick look around and then get the forensic people to do a more thorough job. This security firm that Damien Chase hires, are they any good? Do you ever see them?"

"Very rarely. One of them came for a sandwich the other day but he didn't linger. Some other bloke called him away."

"Do you know where they're from?"

"I'm not sure. I don't think they're local."

Calladine wrote himself a reminder to look them up when he got back to the nick. He went off in search of Rocco. Fifteen minutes later he'd been several times all around what he could get to of the mill, but there was no sign of the DC. Then he heard a loose fence panel rattle. He gave it a shove and a small gap opened. He squeezed through and walked to the rear of the building.

It was much like the front, but there were a number of outbuildings and a fire escape leading up to the top floor. "Rocco! DC Rockliffe!" There was no answer.

"Can I help?" A female voice spoke softly behind him.

Calladine spun around. "Who are you? What are you doing here? It's out of bounds, so I'm told." He showed the young woman his badge. She was dressed in denim jeans, a sweater and a pair of leather boots to her knees. "You're the young woman who spoke to Sergeant Bayliss yesterday."

"I'm Lauren Steele's sister, Lindsey. I come as often as I can and yes, I did speak to your colleague. She said she'd help. Someone needs to do something. My sister is missing and no one cares, certainly not the police."

"Sergeant Bayliss is helping. She's looking into the case as we speak." He certainly wasn't going to tell her about the skeleton, though.

"Your constable will have got lost. There are six floors in there, but you can only access two of them. The corridors twist and turn and it's dark. You can soon lose your way."

"In that case I'd better go and find him."

"Be careful! It's dangerous. Why have you come back? Are you looking for Lauren?"

"No. I'm working on something else."

"You need to search this place for evidence. I can't do it on my own."

"Evidence of what? What makes you think Lauren is here?"

"I don't think she's here now, but she was, I'm sure of it. You need to find out what happened to her."

"Was she living in the camp?"

She folded her arms and looked away. "I don't know. It's possible. But no one there has seen her."

"Why did she run? Had something happened?"

Lindsey Steele shook her head. "I don't think so, but she had met someone, a man. He turned her head, and she became obsessed. She's a pretty girl. I think she attracted the wrong man and now she's paying for it."

"What makes you think she was here?" A girl who looked like Lauren would stand out. If she'd come to the camp, Cerys Powell would certainly have remembered her.

"Lauren was here, Inspector, and something bad happened to her. This whole place is evil. You can feel it as soon as you enter. It should be razed to the ground."

It was an odd thing to say. Calladine recalled the homeless man just now saying the place was cursed.

"Have you seen or heard anything while you've been poking about?"

"No, it's too dark. It would be very easy to have an accident in there and never be seen again. And there is always loud music playing. The security people."

"You've obviously been inside, but I thought the building was locked up?"

"Yes, but there are ways in. That door over there in the corner has a dodgy lock. But like I said, you can't go any further than the second floor. As you can see, there are four more floors above that."

Useful information. "I'll see what I can do, but your sister isn't the reason why I'm here today. I'm not working on that case."

"You can't leave it! You have to do something. I promise you Lauren was here."

"Do you have any proof?"

She held out a see-through plastic bag. "This is my proof, Inspector. It's Lauren's locket; she always wore it — it was a sort of good luck charm. I found it inside there earlier today." She nodded towards the door in the corner. "It was lying on the floor just inside, wedged between two flagstones."

Chapter 12

Mirela was exhausted. He'd kept her out all night. She only knew because dawn was breaking as they drove back. The van was dark but she'd seen the light through the back windows. Mac had taken her to a club somewhere. She had a vague recollection of a bulky doorman, and music playing. He'd taken her to the bar and made her drink a brandy that was laced with something to knock her out. She didn't remember much after that, just stumbling on the stairs as Mac took her to a room.

The flashbacks were terrifying, they were so clear. The room had been empty apart from a bed pushed up against the wall. She closed her eyes and could smell it again. The mattress was filthy. He'd thrown her down and told her to wait. Her shoulder was bruised from where she had bounced against the wall. But she had other bruises too, and a bad headache.

There had been a number of men. When she closed her eyes she could still feel their hands all over her, their breath on her face. She felt sick. She desperately wanted to wash herself clean. What she'd give to be able to wallow in a tub of hot soapy water! But she didn't even have a mattress to rest her weary bones.

This wasn't going to stop. He'd continue to put her through this torture every night until she died. Meanwhile she'd be here in this dark, cold space, alone and desperate for help. She closed her eyes and dozed.

The sound of Mac's voice woke her. He was outside the locked door, talking to someone.

"I want my money! I can't operate like this. If you want things done, then you have to pay." A few moments of silence and then he resumed, cursing. "You bastard! You haven't got a clue. It's not that simple. It has to be carefully set up."

"You'll do as you're told. You work the girls, you collect and you deliver. Even you can manage that."

"The police have been here. What if they find something?"

"They won't. They are looking into something else. We carry on and you do your job. If I say someone has outlived their usefulness, we get rid. Take that tasty little blonde, for example. I asked you to sort her."

Mirela stood with her ear to the door, listening. It sounded like a scuffle.

"Don't even try, sunshine."

"I can't do that. She doesn't deserve it. It's not what I signed up for."

"She upset a valuable client so she had to go. You're too squeamish, that's your problem. I say get rid and all you have to do is grab that crowbar and get on with it. It's easy. You've seen how it's done."

Mirela's heart was thumping. This was murder they were talking about. The key turned in the lock and her heart pounded harder.

"Who have you got for me? I fancy someone special."

They stood in the doorway. She could see Mac but not the other one. He was in the shadows.

"She'll do. Small, slim and I like the hair. Deliver her later. You know where." The man disappeared.

"Stupid man, he's never satisfied. And you let me down. A lump of meat is how the punters described you. It's not good enough, Mirela. That's not what they expect. It's not what they pay for."

"What do you expect when you drug me? But if you don't, then I'll talk, and that scares you, doesn't it, Mac?" She faced him with her hands on her hips, her eyes narrowed and her chin raised.

He dragged her to her feet. "You need teaching a lesson. He won't stand for it. You need to learn that your place is to obey. It doesn't do to answer back, Mirela. Cocky little slut, aren't you?"

The stillness while he held her didn't last long. His fist broke in, smashing the side of her face. The next blow went to her belly, winding her, sending her reeling across the concrete floor. He followed with a series of kicks, a harsh blow to the head and then everything went black.

* * *

"How do you know it belongs to Lauren?" Calladine asked.

Lindsey pointed to the photo. He saw the locket, or one very like it, around the girl's neck. "I recognised it. Mum bought it for Lauren's birthday and it has her initials on the back."

"You're quite sure it's hers?"

She nodded.

"I'll have to take that, Lindsey. I'm sorry."

"Yes, I know. I would have handed it in . . . This place needs searching thoroughly."

"It'll be done, don't worry. You've done a good thing. Is there anything else I should know?"

She shook her head.

"As I said, I'm not here because of Lauren, but I will have this place searched now. We're investigating two possible murders. Two of the homeless men are missing."

"Could that be related to my sister's disappearance?"

"I wouldn't think so."

"Sir?" Rocco came in through the door with the dodgy lock and nodded at the girl.

"I can't find anyone in there. The place is like a rabbit warren, but it seems empty to me, unless security are on another floor. And that music would drive me insane if I had to stay here for any length of time."

"The security office is on the first floor corridor," Lindsey told them.

"There was an office with a frosted glass door, but it was locked up tight."

"C'mon Rocco, we'll go and talk to Cerys."

Lindsey thrust the photo of her sister at him. "Take this, Inspector. It won't do any harm to ask about her while you speak to the people here. They might be more inclined to talk to you."

They left her standing there.

"What's all that about?"

"A missing girl. Ordinarily we'd leave it to uniform, but after the body last night and what that young woman has just given me, I can't see how we can."

"You think this is related to the missing men?"

Calladine shrugged. It was the same thing Lindsey had asked him. This case got more complicated with every passing hour.

* * *

Eddie Potts and another man were standing at the far side of the mill, shouting.

"You can't do the simplest thing, can you?" Eddie was holding the man up against the mill wall, his fist poised to land one on the stranger's chin. "I should take your fucking lights out!"

Calladine and Rocco walked towards them.

"What's going on? What's your problem?" Calladine grabbed Eddie's arm and pushed it down.

"It's nothing, mate. Misunderstanding about access to the mill, that's all."

"Why, what's it got to do with you? There's a security company to look after things. Who are you anyway?"

"Childers. I am security. We don't like folk wandering about. This idiot will get us all into bother."

Calladine released Eddie, whose face was red with anger.

"Sorry. I didn't know the rules had changed," he mumbled.

Childers cautioned him. "You don't go in there again, understand? I'm told it's dangerous. Once more and Chase will move the lot of you on, legal or not."

"Do you people have CCTV footage of this place?" asked Calladine.

"Chase reckons it's not worth it. We get some bother from kids, but nothing serious. So it doesn't justify the added expense."

So much for that. "You okay, Mr Potts?"

Eddie Potts nodded at Calladine and walked across to Cerys, who'd been watching from the food counter. She put her arms round him and looked angrily at Childers, who was moving away.

"Something's not right, Rocco. Why so riled about folk nosing around? What is it they're hiding? And that young woman, Lindsey Steele, was wandering around back there. She didn't say anything about being stopped."

"So why would Potts set about the bloke?"

"Because I think that little spat was about something else. I've no idea what, but those two are up to something. We'll need to keep an eye out."

"Where now, sir?"

"I want to have a quick word with the officer who's watching this place."

No one looked at them as they walked across the yard and spoke to the officer.

"Trouble is we don't know what's of interest. But we think one of them had a camera, so that's a start. It'll be hidden; it was possibly expensive, so use your imagination." They surveyed the jumbled mess the two men had left behind.

"Right, Rocco. We'd better go and see Julian at the Duggan. He said he'd have something for us today."

* * *

"I got nothing from the comb, Inspector. In order to obtain DNA from hair the root has to be present."

"So we still don't know if the arm belonged to Snap or not?"

"Not so. It was his. Both the arm and the blood on the coat belonged to one Stuart Langton. He is your 'Snap', I believe."

Calladine nodded.

"His DNA is on record — an altercation in an Oldston street some six months ago. He was accused of stealing but the case came to nothing. His DNA was taken but couldn't be matched to the traces found at the robbery."

"Any idea how the arm was removed?"

"Brutally." Julian made a sweeping movement with his own arm. "I'd say they used a machete or something like it."

Rocco winced.

"Is there anything on the bloodied rag from the skip yet?"

"As you thought, the blood was from Ronald Weatherby. The DNA matched the blood sample the doc took at the medical centre."

"Thanks, Julian, that's great work. All we have to do now is find the bodies and who it was that did this." The problem was — where to start? "Did the forensic people find anything else — on the road, for example?"

"Nothing that's going to help you, Inspector. We know that Langton was attacked by the dustbin, but Weatherby was not attacked near the skip you found the blood in."

"Great. We know who they are but we're still at square one."

"Do you have anything on the skeleton yet?" Rocco asked.

"Now that is interesting." Julian led them into the morgue across the corridor from his lab.

No sign of Natasha Barrington, Calladine noted.

"The skeleton is that of a female, but getting her age is proving tricky without more tests."

"Why? What's the problem?"

"Like I said, more tests are needed but I suspect she suffered from kidney disease."

"Why would you think that, Julian?"

"In the first instance because of this, Inspector." He handed Calladine a plastic bag containing a thick rubber band. "It was round her wrist. People wear these to support research into a number of diseases. This is a kidney disease awareness bracelet. It hasn't rotted much. If she did have kidney disease, then she'll have attended clinics, perhaps needed dialysis or even have been on the transplant register."

"Thanks, Julian, that's useful. It's a starting point at least."

"There is something else, Inspector. Additional lettering has been added to the bracelet. It's a little worn but I think it's a name."

"Can you write it down — or give me a copy?"

"I need to clean the thing up first. I'll text you."

"I don't understand," Rocco asked. "How does kidney disease lead to you not being able to age her?"

"Having healthy kidneys helps keep your bones healthy. They ensure you have the correct amounts of phosphorus and calcium in your body. When your kidneys don't work effectively, too much phosphorus can build up in your blood. This can cause your body to take calcium from your bones, making them weak. It can be crippling if it's not monitored."

"That gives us something to go on." Calladine looked down at the bones. They'd been carefully arranged on the table, in the correct configuration. He was no expert, but it looked complete.

"I will confirm my suspicions once I've done the tests, Inspector. I'll also look a little closer at the sack she was found in. Nothing obvious has presented itself but I need to do some more tests on the fabric."

"Thanks, Julian. In the meantime I'll have the team trawl the hospitals. Maybe there's a dialysis patient missing."

"I'll see you tomorrow at the Wheatsheaf. Are you bringing Aunt Amy?"

"Sore point. She's dumped me." Rocco looked at him sharply.

"Ah, Cornwall. She's taking my mother — her sister — with her for a while. So I'm losing out too."

"She never gave a single hint; just dropped the bombshell and didn't bat an eyelid."

"That's Aunt Amy; she's a law unto herself. If I'm honest, I couldn't see it working out between the two of you. She's like a butterfly; never still."

Calladine shot him a look. Butterfly wasn't the word he'd have chosen right now.

"So who will you bring? Not that you need to bring anyone, of course."

"Going somewhere, Julian?"

It was Natasha Barrington.

"A drink in the Wheatsheaf, Saturday night."

"Come along," said Calladine. "You'll be more than welcome. You can meet the rest of my team and the doc; he used to do your job."

She beamed at him. "Thanks, Tom. I'd like that."

Calladine's phone rang. The caller was Rhona Birch. Now what?

"Inspector Calladine, I want you back immediately. Get DC Rockliffe to drive and make sure you come straight here."

"Can I ask why? Has something happened? Is it to do with the case?"

There was a long pause.

"Something has happened, Inspector, but not to do with the case."

She rang off. "Birch, being all mysterious. We have to go in right away. She who must be obeyed . . ."

Chapter 13

Ruth had backache. So much for resting, she thought bitterly. Standing up, she put her hands on her hips and arched her back. Another two months or so and it would be over. She couldn't wait. She wanted her old body back. She'd never complain about it again — what was the odd pound or two after looking like a beached whale for months on end?

Lauren's laptop sat on her desk in the corner of the room. A constable from the nick had got it for her within an hour of her conversation with Mrs Steele. She was supposed to be having a hot bath and a nap. But she couldn't resist: the laptop was calling out to the detective in her.

Seconds later she was into Lauren's Facebook account. The girl had left herself logged in, so it was easy. Ruth scrolled through the posts, all historical and all about nothing. No mention of a 'Mac'. Perhaps her mother had got it wrong. Then she clicked on the messages folder and there they all were, entire conversations going back months, and all from him. He was quite a charmer. The conversations were peppered with compliments. He liked her hair. He liked the new dress she'd bought. He wished her well with the exams and promised her a present when she'd completed them.

Last year, in the second week of November, he'd suggested they meet up. Ruth could tell from Lauren's replies that she wasn't too keen. He'd written that he was in London — but she didn't have money for the train. He said he'd help. He said if she came, he'd show her a good time, take her to a show, and she'd stay at a posh hotel. None of it would cost her a penny. Ruth felt her hackles rise. This was grooming, pure and simple.

Lauren had sent him a photo of her with her sister. She'd said she couldn't leave until the New Year because her mother was ill. He'd been annoyed, and there was nothing from him for several weeks. *If only she'd let it drop*, Ruth thought. But she hadn't. There was one more message, telling him how fed up she was. Apparently Lauren had had a crap New Year and had decided that she wasn't going back to college. She wanted out. She wanted to see him.

* * *

"Inspector Calladine. My office," Birch said.

He had no idea what this was about. The woman had a knack for making him feel like a naughty schoolboy and he was racking his brains, wondering what he'd done wrong.

"Sit down. I'm told that this will come as quite a shock, so naturally I didn't want to be the one to have to tell you. But I am your senior officer so, like it or not, the task fell to me."

Now he was scared. Her face had softened, and it didn't suit her. She coughed. "There's no easy way to say this, so I'll just get on with it."

A few moments of uneasy silence ensued, and then:

"This afternoon, at the shopping centre in Gateshead, Lydia Holden was shot dead."

Calladine squinted slightly as he looked at her. Was she joking? His head was full of noise. He shook it, but it wouldn't clear. He couldn't have heard her right. What was Lydia doing in Gateshead for a start? It made no sense. What Birch had just told him had to be some sort of joke, and it was in very poor taste. No, it must be a mistake.

He smiled at her. "Lydia's fine. Lydia's always fine — she's that kind of woman. You don't know her like I do."

"No, Inspector — er, Tom. Lydia is dead."

It still didn't make any sense. Why would anyone want to shoot Lydia? Then it hit him like a kick in the guts. He stared at Birch, and rose from his chair. This was what Marilyn had been trying to warn him about. "Fallon!"

"Yes, Tom, we think so. In fact we're pretty sure. A targeted attack."

He said nothing.

"As you know, Lydia was to be a key witness for the prosecution at his forthcoming trial. This is the way he operates; he has people taken out so they can't testify."

She was right there. He was up on his feet, and every nerve in his body was burning in sheer hatred for that man. The feeling was so strong that he couldn't stand still. He paced up and down Birch's office, trying to process what she'd told him. "I want to see him."

"Out of the question. Now sit down and listen. You are also an important witness. Slanting the evidence a certain way notwithstanding, you are the one person who can put him down for good . . ." She paused; he was still pacing. "You will be placed in immediate witness protection, and your daughter also."

Calladine shook his head. It was a ludicrous idea. "I'm in the middle of a case. I've got two missing men, probably murdered, and the skeleton of a girl. I'm going nowhere until I've sorted that little lot."

"Inspector Calladine, I don't think you appreciate the danger you're in. Fallon's hitman will already have you in his sights. It could come at any time. There'll be no warning and you won't be able to stop it. If you don't do this, you'll be dead too."

"How did he organise it? He must have smuggled a phone in. Can't those damn guards at that prison get anything right?"

Calladine left the room, slamming the door behind him. He was shaking. Whether in rage or fright, he didn't know.

"Joyce. Find everything you can on Childer's Security."

"Are you okay, sir? You look a bit pale."

"I'm fine. Rocco about?"

Imogen looked up. "He's down in the evidence room. Uniform brought in all the stuff they took from the tent."

Calladine strode off to join him. If Snap did have a camera, he wanted to see what was on it.

"Tom!"

It was Jo, his daughter Zoe's partner.

"Do you know where she is, Tom? I'm going out of my mind with worry."

"It's to keep her safe: witness protection. But it won't be for long, I promise you."

"Why? I don't understand. Why would Zoe need protecting — from what?"

"Look Jo, the less you know the better. It's me the bastard really wants, not Zoe, but she's a weak point where I'm concerned. That's why she needs protecting."

"You're talking about Ray Fallon, aren't you? His case is coming up, Zoe told me. You will have to give evidence. Is that what this is all about?"

"I'm sorry, Jo, but I can't talk about this now. I'm up to my neck in work and I've got to get on."

The truth was he had tears in his eyes and he didn't want her to see them. Lydia was dead. He'd once thought he might spend the rest of his life with her. Jo and Zoe knew Lydia too. He would tell them, but he couldn't do it now. He'd break down completely. Lydia had been one of the few women he'd really loved, for a short while. She had looked after him when Fallon had tried to kill him that last time, when he'd shot him in the arm. She hadn't deserved to die like that.

He went into the room where Rocco was examining Snap's belongings. "Anything?"

"Just a load of old tat. No camera. If Snap did have one, then he kept it somewhere else."

"He would have had one, I feel sure of it. He was a photographer. He couldn't just give it up, even when he hit the skids."

"He could have sold it. He'd have needed money."

Rocco was right.

"What now?"

Calladine shrugged. He couldn't think; his head was too full of Lydia. "I'll ask Cerys to look for us. She won't arouse suspicion."

"I'll ask in the second-hand shops in town," said Rocco. Calladine's phone rang. Julian.

"Inspector, half-grown wisdom teeth, so your skeleton is that of a young woman, say between seventeen and twenty-four. Given her age, there was a definite problem with her bones. A blunt trauma to the head caused a skull fracture that led to her death. The blow may not have been intended to kill her, but given her condition it did."

More good news. "Thanks, Julian. Let me know if there's anything else."

"Her teeth were very well looked after, Inspector. Given the state of her bones, that would have meant regular dental visits, so you might try dental records."

Yes he would, but which dentist?

"Incidentally, the name on the bracelet is 'Tracy.' It's a start, at least."

"So, good teeth, young with kidney problems and called Tracy? Thanks, Julian. If you get anything else, let us know."

He turned to Rocco. "She was clobbered on the head. You heard the bit about the bracelet. Can't say it helps much, but it's something. It would help if we knew the place where she was shoved into the sewage system."

"Could be anywhere. That storm last night shook everything up."

They went back to the main office. Imogen had already put some of the details about the girl on the board. Calladine added the facts Julian had just given him.

"Anything on the sewers?"

"I've found a map online, but the pipes are like a maze. They run all over the place. Some are old — Victorian — but a lot are newer."

"She was found on the High Street."

"That doesn't help, sir. In fact it just makes it worse. The main sewer tunnel runs under the High Street, then straight on down to the sewerage works at the back of the canal. But there are dozens of offshoots, going in all directions."

Calladine closed his eyes. He couldn't think straight. He couldn't do this right now. "I'm going home for a bit. I'll be back later." He snatched up his coat and made for the door.

His team just looked at each other.

* * *

He decided to walk. He wanted to find whoever had done this to Lydia and make them pay. Grief was rapidly turning to rage, but he felt helpless, trapped. His job and the trial meant he couldn't go near Fallon. Even if he could get to see him, the bastard would laugh in his face.

Back in his own sitting room, he rang Ruth and told her what had happened.

"I can't work with you or the others for the time being. I'm far too dangerous to be with."

"You're a bloody fool! You should do as Birch told you and go into witness protection. I'm really sorry about

Lydia and I know how hard it will have hit you, but you have to look after yourself."

"The case comes to court next week, but the bastard will try everything in the book to delay it. I can't live like that. Anyway, there's our own cases to think of."

"There's always a case, Tom; it's what we do. Your safety is far too important to compromise like this. My advice is, do what you're told. The rest of us will pick up the slack."

"I'll think about it," he lied. "In the meantime, the skeleton is unlikely to be Lauren Steele. The girl in the sewer had kidney problems and it looks like she was called Tracy."

"Lauren had met a man online. She might have simply run off with him. Superficially it looks like grooming, but he could be genuine. Goes by the name of 'Mac.' The same thing could have happened to Tracy."

"The fact that the skeleton isn't Lauren Steele gives us a huge problem. Not only do we still have to find her, make sure she's safe, but we've got the problem of identifying the skeleton. Speaking of which, the arm did belong to Snap Langton. DNA tests confirmed as much this afternoon."

"Anything on Ron?"

"Not yet. For the time being I'll settle for finding the rest of Snap."

"The sewers I'd say."

"You know what this means, don't you?"

"No. What?"

"The two deaths — Snap and the girl — they could be linked somehow, given that they both ended up in the sewage system."

"Snap and Ron were homeless. They were living in the tented village. Lauren wasn't. She had a good home life. They were male, she's young and female. Big differences, Tom."

Ruth was right. The skeleton girl had well-kept teeth. That didn't sound like someone who was homeless either. "Still, keep it in mind. We've no idea what's at the back of this, and we've no motive. So until we have, we'd best keep an open mind."

"Looks like you'll have to organise a search then."

"I'm trying to put it off, but it'll no doubt come down to that."

"Glad I'm not in. No avoiding it — one of you will end up going down there."

"I'll see if the water people have one of those robot things first."

"It's just a thought, but have you considered going to stay with Eve until this business with Fallon is over? He doesn't know about your relationship with her, does he?"

"It wouldn't be fair to drag her into this. Don't worry about me, Ruth. I'll be fine."

There was a knock at the front door.

"Got to go. I'll ring tomorrow."

It was Mrs Frasier from next door. She had a parcel in her hand.

"I took this in for you, Tom. It came this afternoon."

He wasn't expecting anything. He took it carefully and thanked her. Once she'd gone he put it on the table. For a moment he thought it might contain bones like the ones delivered to the camp, but the packaging was different. There was no postmark. Hand delivered then. It could be from Fallon.

He had no choice but to ring the DCI. Within the hour two forensic people from the Duggan had put the box into a metal casket. They carried it outside and placed it securely in the back of a van. Hot on their heels came Rhona Birch.

"You did the right thing," she told him. "Perhaps now you'll take the offer of protection a little more seriously."

"There could be anything in that. It's not guaranteed to be a bomb, you know."

"And if it is?"

"You tell me how I am supposed to sort this case if I'm banged up somewhere, with no access to anything or anyone?"

"I'll help. Hand it over to me. I do have experience, you know."

"Look. If what's in that box turns out to be something dangerous, then, yes, I'll agree, but if not I carry on."

"Is there anywhere else you could go in the meantime? Somewhere Fallon doesn't know about?"

Calladine heaved a sigh and shook his head. She'd been banging on about witness protection, and now she wanted him to sort himself. She was waiting for him to suggest a place and he nearly did, but something stopped him.

"Come on, there must be somewhere. A safe place you can stay for a day or so?"

He looked at her and Amy's words flashed through his head. *'Beware a woman in authority — she sups with the devil.'* He clammed up. He wasn't going to tell Birch anything further. Well, nothing she could use to trap him. Fallon had to be getting his information from someone, and Birch was an unknown quantity.

"I'll stay with a friend," he lied. "He doesn't live in Leesdon — nothing to do with the police." He tried to smile.

"I'll have to know where you are. I can't just let you go walkabout."

"I'll ring you once it's settled. For now, I'll move into my mother's old place. It's just up the street. Number forty-two. The place is empty. The landlord is doing it up before he lets it again. No one will think of looking there." Of course, he had no intention of actually going there.

"You'll be on the same street still. It's risky."

"Give me an hour or two and I'll sort something more suitable."

"That's not how it works, Inspector."

Before he had the chance to reply, her phone rang. Birch went outside to answer it, giving him a moment to think. If she was right, and he'd no reason to believe she wasn't, he had to disappear. Fallon always hired the best. If there was a contract out on him he was as good as dead. The thought sent his head spinning. Fallon had tried once before and had failed only because of Lydia's intervention. Tears welled in his eyes again.

Birch called to him from the door. "I'll leave a uniformed officer with you. You have a couple of hours to sort this. Just let me know where you're going."

Calladine nodded. A couple of hours was all he needed.

Somewhere in a drawer was an old pay-as-you-go mobile that had belonged to his mother. He had to make some phone calls but he didn't want them traced. After a good twenty minutes of searching he finally found it. The thing was ancient but at least it had been stashed away with the charger. He plugged it in — there was still some credit on it.

"Doc! I can't say much now but I need your help. I'm coming round to yours tonight and I'll want to stay but don't tell a soul, not even the folk from the nick."

He packed a few things and left by the back door so the uniform wouldn't see him. The doc lived on the other side of Leesdon. He couldn't take his car; it was parked out front. He'd go on foot. He needed the thinking time anyway.

Half an hour later, he was in the doc's sitting room holding a glass of scotch. "Basically I'm on the run," he joked. He'd decided not to tell the doc about Lydia yet. He couldn't face it. "I don't want the team to know because Birch will come down heavy on anyone who doesn't play ball with her. I don't know why but I just don't trust the woman. Daft as it sounds, I don't think she's entirely straight."

"All I know about her is that she gets rid of people. What are your plans, Tom?"

"I need to find out who killed the two homeless men. The answer is somewhere in that camp. I need the folk there to talk to me. They wouldn't talk to DI Calladine, but perhaps they'll loosen up for plain old Tom."

"You're planning to join them?"

"Why not? Who's going to think of looking there? Cheers, Doc."

Chapter 14

Friday

"So where is he?"

"I've no idea," said Rocco. "The DCI went round to his place last night and after that he scarpered. I know he doesn't like the woman, but isn't that going a bit too far?"

"He'll have his reasons," said Imogen.

"The problem is she won't let it drop. Birch has been in here half a dozen times already, asking if he's been in touch. I don't think she believes me when I tell her he hasn't."

"Have you asked Ruth?"

"Birch has. Apparently Ruth's coming in today, so we can ask her ourselves."

"This just isn't like him."

"Tell me about it. He's chancing his arm if you ask me. Birch won't stand for it."

"We could try his mobile," said Joyce.

"Done that. Switched off."

"Something's up, got to be. I just wish he'd said something before he went solo."

Ruth walked into the office, throwing off her coat. "Any news?"

They shook their heads.

"We were hoping you'd know something," said Imogen.

Ruth put her bag away in her desk drawer and sat down. She felt weary. If it wasn't for this she'd have stayed at home. "He hasn't contacted me and hasn't said anything to Amy either. She's as puzzled as we are."

"Has something happened?" said Rocco.

Evidently the team didn't know. Ruth looked around at them — she'd leave the part about Lydia until another time. "We think that Fallon wants him dead. He's probably in witness protection." They were obviously surprised but seemed to accept it.

"Julian rang earlier. He wanted Calladine but he'll settle for you."

Ruth picked up the phone.

"Has he turned up yet?"

"No, Julian. But if he contacts you, tell him to ring me. Have you got anything?"

"He received a parcel at home yesterday evening. That could have been what made him flee, though the parcel was innocent enough. Anyway, early results show that it's likely the skeleton belonged to someone with kidney disease."

"And the parcel? What was in it, then?"

"Something he'd ordered online, I presume." Julian was giving nothing away.

"Thanks for the update on the skeleton. I'll get the team on it."

It was on the board — the note to contact the hospitals. The trouble was, the only missing person Ruth wanted to find now was Calladine.

"The missing men from the camp," said Imogen. "We now have positive identities. Snap Langton had only been

128

living rough for about six months so I'm doing some research into his background."

Ruth nodded. It might throw up something. "We still don't have a motive. Let's hope it isn't down to some maniac who's hell-bent on targeting the homeless." She walked into Calladine's office and took a sheet of paper from his desk; random notes he'd made about the case. Among them was his query about Childers and Ace Security.

"We went to see Chase the day before yesterday. He's got no time for any of them. He's got a buyer waiting and needs the land cleared."

"What did Calladine say?"

Rocco shrugged. "Not a lot really. He noted that it might be a motive. But it's stretching it a bit. Chase does have the law on his side if he wants the area clearing."

"Before he went AWOL, the inspector was going to organise a search of the sewers, and see if the water people had those robot things with cameras that go down," Imogen told her.

"Would you get on to them? Also, would you look up a firm called 'Ace Security' and a man called Childers who works for them."

"I've done that already," said Joyce. "There's nothing listed for Ace Security. Not on the web or yellow pages or anywhere else. It seems it's just a van and a man — that Childers bloke."

Ruth looked up at the clock. "Let's meet at about one, and see what we've got."

* * *

Cerys Powell smiled at the newcomer. "There's room in the tent at the top, the red one."

"Will I be sharing?"

"'Fraid so. Does that bother you?"

"Suppose it better not."

"We're not a hotel, you know. But we're all this town has got. The alternative to bunking up with us is nights in a shop doorway or a park bench."

It was a sobering thought. He looked around. There were dozens of people hanging about, almost all men. Some were chatting, some squatting on the ground holding cans of lager.

He spoke loud enough for everyone around to hear. "You might know a friend of mine. You'd know him as Snap."

Cerys looked at the ground and almost whispered.

"We think Snap's dead. The police are investigating. We don't know what happened to him."

"I was hoping to meet up. He contacted me, told me some pretty worrying stuff."

"Look, if you knew him and he contacted you recently, then you must tell the police. They don't know what happened to him. Something he told you could be of help."

He backed away shaking his head. "I'm not sure. I don't have anything to do with the law. For a man in my position it can get tricky."

"You have to. Snap isn't the only bloke from here to go missing recently. The camp is edgy. No one knows what's going on. It can't hurt, can it? You having a quick word?"

He looked around. People were watching, waiting for his response. "Okay — if it helps, then I'm cool with that." He picked up his rucksack and began to walk away. He was wearing an old, loose woollen coat to his knees over a ripped hoodie and jeans, with a pair of battered old trainers on his feet. His hair was long, almost to his shoulders and unkempt, and he had a full beard. His face was grubby with ingrained dirt.

Cerys called after him.

"What do we call you? A nickname will do if you're shy!"

130

"Call me Tom. Just Tom."

He'd got away with it. She hadn't recognised him. She'd only set eyes on him a couple of times, but still . . . The man she saw now was a world away from the smartly dressed cop with the short, neat hair and clean-shaven, chiselled features. Doc Hoyle's wife had been a marvel. She'd sorted out the clothes and then got to work on his face and hair. With a wig and false facial hair, courtesy of Leesdon amateur dramatic society, he was all set. With a bit of luck he'd made enough noise back there to stir things up. And he had.

"I knew your friend," a man said gruffly.

"She said he's dead." Tom shrugged. "Pity. I was hoping for a catch-up. Said he knew stuff that could get us both a bob or two, a sure-fire deal. What do I call you?"

"Newt," said the man, throwing a cigarette end to the ground. "So Snap liked to talk, did he?"

"Yeah. He had an old phone and lately he rang me a lot. He told me stuff; why he did a runner from his old life and that."

"Have you spoken to the police?"

"Wouldn't go near that lot if you paid me. But if I want to stay here, it looks like I'm going to have to. The girl back there is keen for me to tell everything I know. I only came here because there was a bob or two in it. Snap was a fool. He must have opened his mouth to the wrong person. If he'd kept quiet till I got here, he might be alive today."

Tom watched Newt's face. He seemed to have touched a nerve. They had reached the allocated tent and he disappeared inside and threw his rucksack on a mattress. Newt followed him in. "I'd think twice about the police if I was you. Folk around here won't like it. You're new, they'll take against you."

"I can look after myself."

Tom looked at the man more closely. He was wearing good quality boots, certainly not hand-me-downs. As he reached up to open the tent flap Tom also noticed his watch — it looked like gold. Whoever Newt was, he was no down and out. He too was acting the part.

"You don't want this lot on your back. Remember that." With that, Newt grunted an expletive and left.

It hadn't taken long. Tom had the man rattled. But he was flying by the seat of his pants. He'd no idea why Snap had run or how, if at all, Newt was involved in it.

He took the mobile from his pocket and rang Julian. "What was in that package?" Tom said softly.

"What were you expecting?"

"A bomb, or something just as deadly."

Julian tutted.

"Isn't that a little dramatic, Tom? I also hear that you've vanished."

"This is no joke, Julian. I've got Fallon on my tail which is why I've disappeared. I can't explain yet, but I don't trust Birch either."

"Ruth rang me earlier. She's worried about you."

"I'll contact her soon but first I've got stuff to do."

"The package contained a camera, Tom. A very expensive digital one, used by professionals. I've printed out the photographs. There were only six of them, but I've no idea what they mean."

It had to be Snap's camera. But who had sent it to him?

"I need to see them. Will you meet me?"

"I take it I'm not to tell anyone?"

"You've got it, Julian. Meet me on Dale Lane. Park up and wait. As soon as you can."

Tom had brought nothing of value to the camp. He put the phone in his coat pocket and emptied his stuff onto the mattress. He'd go find some blankets later. For now he'd have a walk around the camp. As he left the tent a female voice called to him.

"There will be a meal at one. No cost. Cerys does marvels. Also we have a shower block and toilets over there against the mill wall."

Tom looked at the woman. He guessed she was about sixty. Her hair was untidy and her face tanned and weather-beaten. She looked as if she was wearing all the clothes she owned. A woollen hat was pulled over her overgrown, greying hair.

"Stella. You?"

"Tom."

She was in a tent a short way up from his. As they stood talking, he heard a scream.

"She has nightmares. The girl's been through hell, I'd say. She needs more help than either me or Cerys can give her."

"What happened to her?"

"Best not to ask."

"Perhaps I can help."

"No, you can't."

"Why not?"

"Because you're a man. And anyway she doesn't speak much English."

"Where's she from?"

"Romania, I think. She turned up here about a week ago, in a real mess. When she arrived she was black and blue. Someone had given her a real going over."

"Why not go to the police?"

Stella laughed. "They don't want to know. The minute you say you're living here, they turn off."

Cerys Powell came over to them.

"You've rung the police I take it?"

"I had no choice. They're going to send someone round and they asked if you'll hang about till they get here."

"I've got to meet someone but I'll only be half an hour or so. Get them to wait."

"Okay."

Stella disappeared back inside her tent and the screams ceased. He'd get Ruth to send an interpreter round. Here was another displaced girl, and he could do with knowing her story.

Tom strode off towards the track that led eventually onto Dale Lane, passing a group of men huddled around a fire.

"Can I get into the town this way?" "Yes, mate. Through the loose panel in the fence, across the yard then walk along the wire fence for about ten yards, then there's a gap. That track takes you in."

* * *

So much for security. He set off, glancing behind him every so often to make sure he wasn't followed. As arranged, Julian was waiting for him. He drove a four-by-four with tinted windows, so no one would see him once he was inside. He climbed in.

"Sorry about all this cloak-and-dagger stuff, Julian."

"What *do* you look like?"

"Someone who's homeless and down on their luck, hopefully. I don't have much choice. Fallon wants my blood. His trial is coming up and I'm the only one left who can put him away . . . He's had Lydia killed."

All Julian Batho's amusement at his friend's strange get-up was gone in an instant. "I'm sorry, Tom. I didn't realise it was that bad."

"Birch wants me in witness protection. I should jump at the chance, but something's stopping me. I don't know what it is but she's a tricky one to figure. And if I do what she wants I'll never get this case sorted."

Julian handed him a large envelope containing the photos. "I've done my best at enhancing them but they were taken in the dark. I've looked at them on the computer, but it doesn't help that much."

Tom took them out and spent several minutes looking at printed photos. "That's a body he's dragging."

"Down a garden path, I'd say. You see this area? The rough, grassy patch at the end of the garden just through the trees. The next image shows him digging."

It was the man he'd just met in the camp, Newt; there was no doubt about it. "He's buried a body there!"

"The photos suggest that, yes. The problem is you need more than a few photos before you can do anything. Do you even know where it is? We have a back garden and a possible body, but it could be anywhere."

"There's a photo of a street here. Imogen might be able to do something with it. It's a lead, at least. This is what made Snap run. He must have seen what was happening, photographed it and then had Newt on his back. Perhaps he was spotted, or tackled the bloke. He'd have known that if this man had killed once then he was quite capable of doing it again. Newt followed him here and silenced him for good."

"You need the team to look at this. The first victim — Snap; you need to know where he came from, where he lived and go from there."

"You're right. If Ruth's back at work she'll be at the camp soon. I told Cerys Powell that I knew Snap from old and she had no choice but to let them know at the nick. I'll give Ruth these and get them started."

"If you need anything else, let me know. I will be discreet — I won't even tell Imogen."

* * *

"Ruth! I've just had the desk sergeant on from downstairs," Joyce told her. "Cerys Powell has a new one at the camp. Whoever he is, he knew Snap Langton and he knows about his past."

Ruth put down the paperwork she'd been reading and stretched. "At last. Someone who might give us something. Rocco, you can come too. We'll stop off at Tom's first and check everything's okay."

She was hoping that he might have left something, some clue as to what he was doing.

"Has Birch said anything else?" said Rocco.

"No, but she's not happy. Tom isn't in witness protection, he's gone AWOL. If he doesn't let her know where he is soon it'll be the end of his job. I really don't understand what he's up to; it's not like him. He always stays in touch."

"I don't understand either."

"He's got some weird idea about not trusting Birch. But keep this under wraps. Not a word, not even to Imogen."

They soon pulled up outside Calladine's house. Rocco switched off the engine.

"Uniform's still here," he said, and spoke to the man standing by the door. "Have you seen anything? Has he been back?"

"No, Constable."

"Is the door open?"

"Yes."

"We'll have a quick scout round. Look in all the rooms — and there is a cellar," said Ruth.

While Rocco moved around the house Ruth stayed in the lounge. It all looked as if Calladine had just stepped out of the room. Ruth saw that his mobile and wallet had been left on the coffee table. She knew he wouldn't go anywhere without them. On the other hand there was no sign of a struggle. That was something at least.

Rocco came back. "He's not here. But the back door is ajar. He must have left that way, gone onto the road at the top. The copper on the door would have been none the wiser."

"In that case he could have been gone since last night. Bloody fool on the door should have checked on him regularly. Tom's mum lived a few doors up and the house is still empty. We'll check there before we go to the camp."

The two detectives walked up the street. Ruth tried Freda Calladine's front door — it was open and she peered in. "This isn't right, Rocco." The place had been ransacked.

"Get the uniform up here."

There wasn't much of Freda's stuff left. Tom had taken anything personal but what furniture was left had been broken up and every room had been trashed. Paint had been thrown at the walls, splattering over everything.

Angry now, Ruth asked the copper, "Didn't you see or hear anything? Inspector Calladine checks on this place every day. The landlord is here redecorating most of the time, so this was done within the last twelve hours."

"Whoever did this must have been looking for the inspector," said Rocco.

"And got bloody annoyed when they couldn't find him. We have no choice now, we'll have to ring the nick and tell them what's happened. They'll get CSI round but I bet they don't find much."

"Someone's pretty keen to find him, aren't they, Sergeant?"

"Let's hope for his sake they don't succeed."

Chapter 15

Ruth and Rocco were waiting for him when Tom returned to the camp. From Ruth's expression he knew at once that she'd twigged. Rocco, however, was standing with his back to him, busy talking to some of the other residents.

Ruth hissed at him. "What the hell are you playing at? Birch is livid; I wouldn't want to be in your shoes once she finds you. And your mother's old house has been trashed."

Calladine's face turned pale. He had still hoped he was wrong about Birch, but this proved that his instincts had been right. He led Ruth around the side of the mill, where they wouldn't be seen.

"You know I've got Fallon on my case. Well, I received a package last night, delivered by hand. I thought it was a bomb! Birch wants me in witness protection, but I don't trust her. Last night she came round to the house. I told her I'd think about it and while I made up my mind, I'd stay in my mum's house. The thing is, I didn't tell anyone else, only her."

"What are you getting at, Tom?"

"I think Birch is on Fallon's payroll."

"No! Surely not? She's grim but I didn't have her down as bent."

"She's the only person who knew where I'd be. I can't go into hiding; it would drive me mad. I'm still cut up about Lydia. I'm better working; it keeps my head straight. The last thing I need is time to wallow around in grief." He was studying the ground, a furious look on his face.

Ruth looked at him and felt her stomach lurch. Lydia's death would have hit him hard. She put her hand on his arm. "This is serious, isn't it? You are the only one left who can put him away. But Birch — I still can't believe it."

"He'd have offered her a fortune. All she'd have to do was set me up. One of his henchmen would do the rest. Marilyn did try to warn me but I thought she was exaggerating. She always was highly strung, given to thinking the worst."

"That's why you're here, isn't it? You're avoiding Birch."

"That and cracking on with the case. Look, I've got these." He handed her the envelope containing the photos. "The package contained a camera, not a bomb. I think this is why Snap ran. You need to find out where he lived. The man in the photos is called 'Newt,' and that's all I've got. He's one of the blokes living here, but I don't think he has any need to live rough. I'm sure he's here looking for Snap. One of the photos shows him with a woman's body. I think Snap witnessed something and was threatened. I think Newt followed him here and finally did him in."

"And Ron? What about him?"

"They were friends. I think the killer is worried that Snap told him. That's why he had to go too."

She stood looking at him, her hands on her hips. "So now you're masquerading as an old friend of Snap's and putting it about that you know stuff too? Not content with having a villain like Fallon after your head, you've now got this other maniac chasing you."

Calladine thought for a few moments. "Yep, that's about it."

"I'll get Imogen on it. She's already done some background research on Snap."

"I want a Romanian interpreter, too. But it has to be a woman — and get her to dress down, look like she might be one of these . . . us."

"What for?"

"There's a girl living here with an older woman who's taken her under her wing. The girl's Romanian and she's scared out of her wits about something. I think she might prove useful."

"You have been busy."

"I want her to talk, tell us what happened to her. Something's not right. Earlier on she was screaming and wailing in her sleep."

"And you? What are you going to do now?"

"Keep my eyes peeled and try to stay out of trouble. Newt has taken an interest in me because he thinks I knew Snap. I need to find out his real name. Everyone uses nicknames here, so it's not easy. 'Newt' will be short for something."

"I take it you're staying undercover for now?"

"Whatever you do, don't tell Birch you've seen me. In fact don't tell anyone."

"I'll head off, then. You disappear and I'll find Rocco and get back to the station."

"I've got my mum's old mobile. Here's the number. Ring me if you get anything."

"Who did your make-up by the way?"

"The doc's wife and these are some of his old clothes."

"She's good."

* * *

Ruth was pinning the photos on the incident board when DCI Birch called out.

"Any word from DI Calladine?"

"No, ma'am."

140

"His caseload? How are you coping?"

"We have a lead, of sorts. With a little more research it could pay off. I'll keep you posted." Ruth turned to look at the woman. To her surprise she was standing in the doorway with the chief super. What on earth was he doing here?

"If you have any idea where he is, you must tell us." He sounded irritated and looked flustered.

"Of course, sir."

"When he does turn up I need to speak to him right away," he added. "Impress upon him that it's urgent, very urgent indeed."

What had got him so agitated? Ruth was staring at him, without meaning to, just thinking, but his face reddened and he couldn't look her in the eye. Something was wrong. This was seriously out of character for the chief super. Not that she knew him well, of course. It was based on everything she'd heard about him.

"Imogen. Would you try and find out where Snap Langton lived?" Ruth handed her one of the photos. "It's already been digitally enhanced but it's still difficult to see. I think that might be the road name there. See? It shows the corner of the house and you can almost see the name, but I can't make it out. If you get anywhere, would you see if there have been any serious crimes nearby during the last six months?"

"Joyce, do we have access to a Romanian interpreter? Has to be a female."

"I could get one organised."

"It's pretty urgent. Where are we with the water people?"

"They do use robot cameras," said Imogen. "They've been used recently down that huge hole that appeared on the dual carriageway in Manchester. I had a word with the bloke who operates it and he said the best place to go in would be the hole in the High Street. That's why it's still causing the traffic bottleneck. Effectively they're waiting for us to give them the nod."

"How much notice do they need?"

"He said to ring him. He can have the equipment there within the hour."

"This afternoon then, at about two."

Joyce called across from the office phone. "Ruth! It's a woman for DI Calladine. Will you take it?"

"Who is this?"

"Eve Buckley. I've been ringing Tom since last night but he doesn't answer. Is everything alright with him?"

How to answer that one? After all, it was his mother asking. She thought for a moment. "He's working undercover. But don't worry. Everything will be back to normal soon."

"I wanted to ask him round for dinner on Sunday. It's nothing special, just a roast with the family and Edwin, my brother. He's been going on about Tom ever since he met him the other night. In fact it was he that suggested something might be wrong. He's been ringing me non-stop all morning, asking if I've found him yet. I thought that rather odd since Edwin is the chief superintendent. Shouldn't he know what his officers are up to?"

"I shouldn't worry. It's only work."

"Well, when he turns up would you ask him to ring me, please?"

Ruth sat back and rubbed her belly. Why would the chief super be so interested in Tom's whereabouts? He'd taken Birch to the Buckleys' birthday bash the other night — perhaps the DCI had asked him to do some prying. But that didn't really cut it. Up until the other night Edwin Walker had hardly known of Tom's existence. He was a name in a file, nothing more. So, apart from learning that he was family, what else had changed?

"I've got an address for Snap Langton," said Imogen. "He lived in a place called Whirley, just outside Macclesfield."

"Great stuff! Any joy with the street name?"

"Jubilee Close, I think. I'm just about to look it up, see if there is such a place."

"Whirley? It's near a place called Broken Cross. It isn't that far," said Rocco. "We could be there within the hour."

"Okay. You and Imogen take that one and I'll take a uniform to the High Street to meet the water people. Joyce, keep trying for the interpreter. Tomorrow morning would be great if you can arrange it. Can we meet back here at about six? Feedback before we go home."

* * *

Birch collared Ruth as she passed by her door on her way out.

"DS Bayliss, you know something. You and Calladine are as thick as thieves. You work closely together, and have done for a long time, so if he was going to confide in anyone, it would be you."

The woman was leaning forward, staring at her, thick arms folded, ample chest resting on the desk top.

"I'm sure he'll turn up."

"Oh so am I, but it's where he is now that's the issue."

"Perhaps he feels it's safer if no one knows where he is?"

"That is why I offered him witness protection. He's a key witness in a headline trial. He's not stupid; he knows he'd be looked after. I don't know what motivated him to disappear but he needs finding, for his own safety. If you are able to speak to him, tell him that, will you?"

"You know his mother's house was broken into?"

Birch looked shocked.

"When?"

"Sometime last night."

Birch stood up, turned her back on Ruth and went to the window. "That's why you won't speak to me. You've spoken to DI Calladine so you know that he told me that's where he'd be."

She was sharp alright. "What do you expect me to say, ma'am? From where I'm standing it appears that you have to be responsible."

She turned back to Ruth. "Well, I'm not. Has he been taken? Answer me that, at least."

"No ma'am, he's quite safe."

"Ruth. I am not the enemy. You have to trust me or this entire DCI thing isn't going to work."

"I'm not sure I can. Calladine told you where he was going, and within a few hours the house was done over, completely trashed. The finger does point directly at you, ma'am."

"I had nothing to do with what happened. You're going to have to leave this to me. Not ideal, and does nothing to reassure you that I'm not guilty, but it's all I've got to offer right now."

Chapter 16

"It'll be set up shortly, and then we'll have a look," the engineer told Ruth. "You can watch from the monitor in the tent. Get out of this rain."

"What does it do?"

"It's a little miracle. A robust remote-controlled camera with tyres that can roll over just about any surface. It's ideal for the sewer system. It can travel some distance too, and that allows us to do a fairly comprehensive check on what's going on down there. It's used for blockages and when sinkholes appear in the roads for no reason. We see all sorts. Hope the odd rat won't scare you."

"Can we try in both directions — up and down the High Street? We've no idea which way the — er — deceased travelled."

"I do know what we're looking for. If you can ignore the rats, I'll try and cope with whatever we might find. And the direction of travel would be east to west — gravity, you see. There's a slight slope."

Fair enough. Ruth settled herself inside the tent in front of the monitor. She had a simplified map of the immediate system. Interestingly, if you followed the sewer eastwards it made its way along the side of Chase Mill.

The engineer called out. "It's going down now!"

Seconds later the main sewer tunnel became visible. The image was grey, but clear enough. Ruth watched, fascinated. It was a window on another world. As her eyes became more focused she could see that she was looking at the Victorian brickwork facing the inside of the tunnel. It looked surprising clean. There was a stream of fast flowing water along the tunnel floor, the result of the recent heavy rain.

The camera inched along. There was a narrow platform to the right, just wide enough for a man to walk along. Periodically there was a channel branching off to the left or the right, but none of them looked big enough to have carried a sack containing a body.

The robot had been moving east for about ten minutes when Ruth saw it. A brown sack was bobbing in the water. It had snagged on a metal spoke sticking out from the platform.

The baby was turning somersaults in her belly and Ruth felt sick, knowing what this might be. She shouted out: "Stop!"

The engineer came back inside. He studied the image on the monitor for a few seconds and shook his head. "There, too. Clothing caught on the metalwork."

Ruth inhaled and closed her eyes. If those two shapes were bodies, how had they ended up down there? "We need to get someone down there to recover the . . . findings."

"Ring your people. I'll keep things as they are until they've had a look."

"And now I need some air."

* * *

Rocco was smiling. "Ruth definitely got the short straw. This is far better than staring at the contents of Leesdon's sewers. Apart from which, I like Cheshire — it's nice and green."

"Nice and expensive, you mean, especially around here. This is prime Premier League footballer territory. Why have you brought us this way? Wouldn't the motorway have been quicker?" said Imogen.

"Doubt it at this time of day. I know this area. At the top of Alderley Edge High Street we swing a left and that'll take us to Whirley. It's just a mile or so from that junction."

"How come you know it so well?"

"I had an auntie who lived in a little village near here called Broken Cross. I was farmed out for the school holidays every summer — used to have a great time. I was something of a wanderer and I'd walk for miles exploring the countryside. We can return via Macclesfield town, making it a round trip."

"And there was me thinking you'd spent all your days in Leesdon."

"Working parents. My auntie lived on a road full of kids my age. I had some great friends around here — still do. Look to your left."

"A car park?"

"A car park for the local beauty spot. That's the actual edge — you know — as in 'Alderley Edge'. There are caves there. We kids used to play in them. We'd walk and spend the day. It's a weird place, something to do with Merlin. We were always looking for him, or King Arthur's knights who are supposed to be sleeping there."

"Wasn't that dangerous — kids and caves? It'd never be allowed today."

"We didn't care, and neither did anyone else I don't think. Auntie didn't have kids of her own so a lot of stuff went over her head. I got away with loads."

"Who'd have thought it? Rocco the tearaway!"

"You and Julian still going strong?" Rocco said.

"Yep, he's really nice, once you get beneath all the science and seriousness. What about you, Rocco? No nice young lady in your life yet?" Imogen teased.

"Could be . . . Not saying yet, though, in case I jinx it."

"You can't get away with that! C'mon — spill. We don't keep things back."

"Calladine does."

"He tells Ruth stuff and she filters it down, but she does leave out the juicy bits."

Rocco grinned. "And there are a lot of juicy bits. I bet we don't get to know the half of it."

"She's very loyal. Ruth wouldn't tell us anything that would show Calladine in a bad light."

"Looks like we're here."

On a small sign at the side of the road was the village name: 'Whirley'.

"Jubilee Close is on a small housing estate. A fairly new one, I reckon. There was nothing here but fields when I was a kid."

"Over there, Rocco. See — 'Jubilee Park'. That must be it."

Jubilee Park was a select development of no more than five short streets. The houses had been built in the last ten years and most of them were detached.

Imogen reached into her briefcase for her notes. "Snap Langton lived at number three."

"I'll park outside."

Number three was a large detached house with two big bay windows, a double garage and a long front garden. The two detectives walked up the drive to the front door and rang the bell. Imogen knew someone was in because she could hear a child's voice. The woman who answered had short blonde hair cut in a bob, and she wore a vivid red lipstick that was hard to ignore. She carried a small child.

"I'm not buying anything."

Imogen smiled and flashed her warrant card. "We're not selling. We're from Leesdon CID. I'm DC Imogen

Goode and this is DC Simon Rockliffe. We'd like to ask you a few questions, if you don't mind."

The woman stuck her head out of the door and looked up and down the close. Worried what the neighbours might think, Imogen presumed.

"You'd better come in."

She led them into a large sitting room with double glass doors that led into a huge conservatory and then out to the garden. She put down the child — a little boy — and he ran off to play with his toys.

"Can I ask your name?" said Rocco.

"Kate Humphries. What's this about?"

"Did you know a man called Stuart Langton?"

"Snap? Why, what's happened to him? He's been gone for months. I've been worried about him, the daft man. He wasn't very well, so when he took off I wasn't really surprised. We argued a lot. He was depressed and not getting any better despite all the pills he swallowed. The relationship was rocky before that, though. When he went I can't say I was surprised, but as time went by I did wonder what had become of him."

She became silent, and after a few moments her face fell. "Is he in trouble? The police don't come knocking on your door for no reason. Has something happened to him?"

"Possibly," Imogen replied, as gently as she could. "We think that Snap has had an accident."

"What sort of accident? Is he okay? Is he in hospital?"

"No. It would really help to clear this up if you could tell us something about him. How you knew him, why he left, that sort of thing."

Kate Humphries sat down and indicated the chairs, looking at each of them in turn. "We weren't married or anything. We went out for a bit. He even lived here with me for a while."

"We thought he had a flat."

"He did. Even after he moved in here he never gave it up. Insurance I suppose, in case we didn't work out. Which eventually we didn't."

"Why was that? Why did he leave?"

"His business failed. Snap was a photographer. For a while he did really well. He did weddings and christenings. He was popular and reasonably priced. Then the rumours started. They weren't true of course, but people weren't so keen after that."

"What rumours?"

"About him dealing drugs to the kids. A neighbour said he'd seen them knocking on the door — my door. He said Snap had taken money off them in exchange for pills."

"And this wasn't true?"

"No. Danny Newton was the man who started it, but he was lying. He used to live next door. He hated Snap for some reason, but I never did get to the bottom of why."

"This Danny Newton, do you know where he is now?"

"He disappeared, not long after Snap."

"Do you know where he went?"

"I've no idea and I don't want to either. The man's evil. The house is empty and up for sale, but he and his girlfriend were renting. His girlfriend got fed up with him. He kept mouthing off about Snap and me. One day she gave him an ultimatum. They must have argued. She was crying a lot back then. She used to come round and tell me what a pig he was. One day she was gone. Shortly after that he disappeared too."

Imogen showed Kate a photo. "Did Snap own a ring like this?"

"Yes. His mother gave it to him. It was a lovely ring. It'd been passed down through his family."

"The neighbour's girlfriend — do you know her name?"

"Gwen Bracewell. She was nice; we became quite close. She used to look after my boy Louie for me when I had to work late. I'm really surprised she never got in touch after she left. I have tried to ring her but her mobile doesn't work anymore."

Imogen and Rocco looked at each other. Imogen was thinking about the photo she'd seen, in which a man was dragging a body down a garden path. Possibly in Jubilee Close.

"Can I look outside? And would you mind if I took a couple of photos?"

Kate Humphries showed them out through the conservatory door. The garden was long. A path ran through the centre with a lawn on either side. At the end of the plot was a stone-flagged area, and then it was open to the woods beyond.

"This is a lovely spot. Nice and private." Imogen wandered around for a few minutes, taking in the layout. Kate had gone to catch up with her son who was banging a stick against some plants.

"This is where Snap hid," Imogen told Rocco. "This Acer is big enough." She pointed to a huge, leafy thing in a large stone pot. "He could have crouched behind here — see. The angle on next door is exactly right. It must have been dark but the neighbour, Danny Newton, spotted him. From that moment, Snap's card was marked."

"Don't you think it's a bit far-fetched?"

"No, Rocco, I don't. We have the photos, we have the exact spot, and Newton and his girlfriend are both missing. I think Newton followed Snap and caught up with him in Leesdon. Snap could have dropped him right in it if he'd wanted to."

"It's certainly a motive. So what now?"

"We'll have to ring it in. Since Calladine's missing we'll have to tell Birch. We need the local forensic team down here to search for Gwen Bracewell's body."

Birch was surprisingly supportive. "Wait there for them. I'll get onto the Macclesfield force and get someone down to relieve you. And well done."

"Are you okay, love? Only you don't look too clever." The engineer handed Ruth a mug of tea.

"I'll be fine in a minute or two. This sort of thing doesn't usually bother me, but lately I find the nitty-gritty stuff stomach-churning."

She'd rung DCI Birch and told her about the find. Birch hadn't sounded too pleased. She'd gone on again at length about Calladine being missing. Said it should be him and not Ruth scavenging around the sewer system.

She was right too. Ruth wasn't up for this, not after what they'd just found. Perhaps it was time to coax him back into the fold. But was he right? Could it really be that their new DCI was on Fallon's payroll? Ruth sipped on the tea. It was a ludicrous idea. Surely stuff like that got checked out?

Julian and the forensic people from the Duggan were on their way. She'd wait until they got here then check in with Imogen and Rocco. After that she'd ring Calladine and bring him up to date. Ruth closed her eyes. She felt dreadful. Perhaps it was finally time to give it up until after the baby.

Eventually the scenes of crime people arrived, suitably dressed. She had warned them that they'd be paddling in the sewers.

Julian winced when he looked at the image on the monitor. "We'll do the recovery, get the body or bodies, if that's what's in the sack, back to the morgue and hand over to Doctor Barrington to do her stuff. We should have something soon. If one of them is Stuart Langton, we already have his DNA on file. You look a little green around the gills, Ruth. Why don't you get off?" Julian looked over at the uniform who was drinking tea outside. "I'll get that young man to watch events in here."

Ruth nodded. She was shattered and needed to lie down. "I'll ring tomorrow. I'll be glad when this one's done."

Chapter 17

It was getting dark and the camp had settled into an uneasy quiet. Calladine could hear dogs barking and somewhere in the distance tin cans were being thrown against a wall. He'd already decided to spend the night at the doc's. If he slept in the camp, there was the risk of being set upon in the dead of night by Newt or some other miscreant chancing his arm. And there was the Hobfield to consider. If the hooligans from there did cause trouble, then the police would be called and that might reveal his identity.

He threw his rucksack over his shoulder and walked towards the track that ran from the back of the mill. It still needed searching, he remembered, making a mental note to tackle that tomorrow. He passed one or two of the others leaning against the red brick wall. They were standing around a fire, drinking beer and sharing cigarettes.

A bearded man called out to him. "Be careful! We're not allowed to go everywhere and especially not back there. Childers, the security bloke loses his cool big time if he catches anyone."

Calladine nodded. The cop in him wanted to know what Childers was hiding. He'd ask Ruth if she could get hold of the plans to this place tomorrow. It'd help to know more about the layout before he had a closer look round.

He snuck through the gap in the fence, out of sight of the others. He was about to climb the small embankment onto the track when he heard voices. Two men were arguing in the shadows cast by a large wooden building tacked on to the rear of the mill.

"I reckon you're up to something. I'm right, aren't I?"

It was Newt's voice. Calladine held himself flat against the wall.

"What if I am? It's got nothing to do with you. Keep out of my business," said the other.

"I might just let her know, that girlie of yours. She could go to the police. So much for romance, eh?"

"You don't know what you're talking about."

"I know what you did. And I know about the bones." Newt had lowered his voice.

Calladine listened intently. He needed to know who Newt was talking to.

There was silence.

"I've worked it out, some of it anyway. You want this place cleared but you don't want to upset that tart of yours too much. What don't you want people finding out? What are you up to?"

"Nothing. You're deluded."

Calladine risked a quick look round.

"Oh no. I'm right, I know I am. You're up to something."

"Nothing. And if you want to stay healthy, keep comments like that to yourself."

Newt poked the other man in the chest. "I know what you keep in there. What do you do with them? You need to watch out or you're going to get caught. That little girlie you've got wouldn't like that, and she won't like what you're doing either."

More silence, and then the other man spoke again. "You're talking rubbish. You must be drunk; you're off your head!"

"I'll tell her. I'll tell Cerys all about what you've been getting up to."

Calladine risked another look. It was difficult in the darkness, but he could just make out the stranger grabbing Newt by the throat, spinning him round and holding him against the wall.

"No you won't or I'll knock your stupid head off. Loser!"

The man with Newt was Eddie Potts. Calladine could just see his face in the dim light from the cloud-covered moon. What was going on? He crept a little closer.

Newt retaliated. He now had a knife and was holding it to Eddie's throat. Calladine knew he had to do something. He was about to jump forward when an empty beer can flew past his ear and clattered across the concrete yard. The men sprang apart.

"Who's there?" Eddie shouted.

Calladine took his chance and lurched forward. "Looking for the track. Bloody holes. Nearly bust my ankle."

It worked; the moment was defused. Newt sidled towards him. Beads of perspiration were visible on his face.

"I'd watch out. This place is a death trap at night." He laughed to himself and turned and walked away.

Calladine called into the darkness. "Alright, mate?"

"Mind your own fucking business. You've no right being back here. Keep disobeying the rules and you lot will be moved on."

"It's Eddie, isn't it?"

"Who are you?"

"Just one of the great unwashed. He was giving you grief, I could see. He's a volatile one, that Newt. You should keep out of his way."

"I intend to."

Calladine made a rapid, calculated guess. "It's the bones, isn't it?"

"What do you mean?"

"You're the one who's been sending them to the helpers." Closer now, Calladine could see the man's eyes narrow.

"You know nothing. I wouldn't go spreading that around if I was you."

Eddie Potts was evidently not what he appeared to be.

"Cerys know, does she?" Calladine probed.

Eddie grabbed Calladine by the front of his coat. "No, and don't you dare tell her either. We've got to go. I'm trying a few scare tactics that's all. The whole bloody camp has to scarper, and fast. If we don't there will be trouble. A few bones in the post will be nothing in comparison to what will happen next, believe me."

"Why are you doing this? Someone got your arm up your back?"

"Just mind your own business. I've got to go." He let go and pushed Calladine back.

"Cerys said the bailiffs had been. So there's no need for scare tactics anymore. They'll do the job for you."

"Not quick enough. Cerys will get it stopped somehow. Before Chase can act she'll have the whole bloody town behind her."

"Whatever happens, Newt's trouble, and now I know what you've done too. You're skating on thin ice, Eddie. Either one of us could tell Cerys."

"I'd shift if I was you. Get caught round here and it won't be pleasant for you. Childers doesn't have the self-control I do."

"What is it you're trying to hide, you and him? Why don't you just tell me, Eddie?"

"Because I've got nothing to tell. Now fuck off and leave me alone."

Calladine saw a van parked up a few yards away. He made out the words painted on the side: 'Ace Security.'

Eddie Potts vanished into the shadows. Calladine needed to speak to Newt. He returned to camp and found him talking to the men still grouped around the fire. He took the can of lager one of them held out to him.

"Nasty piece of work. Security, is he?"

"Sort of. He does a bit of spying for them, I reckon. Someone's giving him a bung to make sure this place is cleared out, that's my theory. Word of advice — don't get involved. He's dangerous."

Calladine took a swig from the can. "I could see that. It's him sending them bones, isn't it? He's Cerys's fella so he must have a bloody good reason to do something like that."

"He wants us gone. He's up to something in that mill, and he doesn't want anyone finding out."

"You have been busy. Do you know what he's up to?"

"I wouldn't say even if I did. Worth money, information like that. You'll have to find out for yourself. I keep my eyes and ears open all the time and I watch. I watch the bloody lot of them."

"Get much trouble from the security people?"

Newt shrugged. "He has to catch me first."

"You've got it all worked out, haven't you?"

"This place has plenty secrets," Newt said grimly.

* * *

DC Becket from the local nick stood at the end of Kate Humphries' garden with his hands in his jacket pockets and a distinctly annoyed expression on his face. "What sort of wild goose chase is this?"

"Sorry to drag you away from your important work. It's just that we thought finding the body that might be buried here could just be a priority." Imogen's tone had more than a touch of sarcasm.

157

"It's the *might be* that's putting us off. You've got nothing, no proof, no evidence, not even a missing persons report. This is going to be a monumental waste of time and money."

"Gwen Bracewell was reported missing by her parents, six months ago. The fact that you chose to ignore it is not our responsibility."

"Just because she's missing doesn't mean she's buried here. You've got the whole works down here on nothing more than a possibility. Look at this lot." He nodded at the flood lights, the uniformed officers carefully going over the ground and the white-clad CSI folk who'd arrived at the scene. "This won't go down well with my DCI."

Imogen felt like punching him. Kyle Becket was young, not bad looking but far too full of himself, with his sharp, expensive suit and his gelled blond hair.

Rocco whispered in her ear. "I hope we're right. The suspense is purgatory. Birch won't be happy either if we mess up."

"We've seen the photos, we've identified the place — the exact spot, mind you. It shouldn't take long."

One of the uniformed officers had a sniffer dog with him, one specially trained to locate human remains. It had done a circuit of the immediate area and was finding a patch under an oak tree particularly interesting. The handler called out to Becket. "The soil has been disturbed at some time. The ground is hard, but there's an indentation."

The other officers moved in and began slowly to dig and scrape the soil away. "Here we go." Imogen pulled a face and moved a little closer.

Kate Humphries kept peeking out of the French doors. She didn't seem at all bothered about the activity next door, and periodically handed out mugs of tea.

"Do you think she knows, or suspects? She's far too matter of fact for my liking. If I thought my neighbour had killed and buried someone in his garden, I'd be distraught. It's almost like she expected this to happen."

"Snap is missing, don't forget. Perhaps she thinks he's involved somehow. We can ask, but I doubt we'll get anywhere," said Rocco.

A whistle was blown by one of the officers who was digging and work stopped. They had something. The CSI team moved in.

Rocco set down his mug of tea on the garden table. "This is it."

Becket walked over to them, looking grim.

"It's a woman. Knifed through the chest by the look of it and badly cut up around the head. Do you know who did this?"

"We think so but we're still building the case. Forensic evidence is key. You get that, and we'll get the perpetrator."

* * *

"Shift yourself."

Mac took hold of Mirela's arm and pulled her to her feet. He was in a bad mood. Things were going wrong. Far too many demands were being made of him and he was losing control. "We're going out. Shower first, a little ride in my car, and then you entertain an important friend of mine. Get it right and I'll sort a mattress for you."

Mirela was terrified. She still ached from the last beating he'd given her. If she got it wrong this time, he'd kill her.

Mac walked her across a darkened room and down some stairs. At one end of the room beyond was a row of showers. They had no doors.

"Get in and clean yourself. My client is fussy."

"Is it the man you brought here before?"

"What if it is? You do as you're told and don't ask questions."

Mirela slipped out of the flimsy dress and turned on the shower. She hoped the water would warm up. She kept putting her hand under it but it stayed cold.

"Move your butt." He stood, looking her up and down.

"I'll freeze!"

"Get in or I'll put you in and drown you, bitch."

The water was so cold it hurt. There was no soap and no towel. After a couple of minutes he threw her a rough hessian sack and told her to get dried.

Mirela's teeth were chattering. The sack scraped her skin, particularly where it was bruised from his punches. His phone rang. The client, she presumed. He'd put out a tight, low-cut black dress for her. Still wet, Mirela wriggled into it. The thing barely covered her hips.

Mac was arguing again. He was shouting at whoever had called him. The man had so much rage. Mirela ran her frozen, blue fingers through her dripping hair. The man was a beast. He was evil and deserved to die.

She watched as he turned his back and walked away from her. He was still ranting, lost in the argument. Mirela looked around the room. There was a lot of junk lying around and her dark eyes alighted on a pile of roughly hewn logs. There must have been some sort of burner or boiler in here at one time.

Could she do it? If she got it wrong, then she'd be signing her own death warrant. But eventually he'd kill her anyway. She crept towards the logs. He was hunched forward, still ranting into the phone.

"I'll sort it. I know what I'm doing. I'll bring the girl. You like her, you said you did. She's young, great body, knows every trick in the book."

He was talking about her. How dare he? Anger gave her courage. Mirela picked up a log and held it aloft. She paused, her heart thumping. Despite the cold, sweat had broken out on her forehead. She closed her eyes, said a little prayer and swung. The sound of the thud resounded in the stone room. Mac staggered forward and then fell flat on his face.

Mirela stood silent, watching him. He didn't move. She'd done it! She raised the log and hit him again, this time across the upper body. "That is for Anna!"

Mirela threw down the log, picked up a screwdriver lying in the junk and left the room, closing the door behind her. She'd no idea where she was or even which floor she was on. Now to find a way out.

Chapter 18

"Snap ran because he witnessed a murder. That's what the photos were all about. The man dragging the body is the prime suspect for Grace Bracewell's murder. A man called Danny Newton. Any ideas?" Ruth was speaking to Calladine on the phone.

"That's the bloke here, the one they call Newt. He's shifty, and I'm sure he's not homeless. He's too well kitted out and he wears a fancy watch. He's the one who took an interest in me when I said I knew Snap. Now I can see why."

"I'm going to get a warrant and have him arrested."

"You'll have to have enough to make it stick."

"For now we'll go with the photos, the neighbour's statement and the fact he's where he is. With any luck the forensic people in Macclesfield will give us the rest soon."

"Okay. Get it sorted with Birch."

"Where've you been all night?"

"Mrs Doc gave me a comfy bed and made me a cooked breakfast this morning. I don't want to go back to the tented village but I've no choice. I'm on my way there now and people are giving me strange looks. I'll be glad when this one's over."

"Me too. I need the downtime." Ruth was making her way up the stairs to the office as she spoke to Calladine. It was becoming more and more of an effort. Soon she'd have to call it a day.

"By the way, I've sorted the bones that were sent in the post."

"Go on, then. Who?"

"Eddie Potts. He's not as affable as he pretends to be. He's a regular roughneck and I'm still working out why. I've got two theories spinning around in my head."

"Go on."

"Theory one is that he's up to something in that mill. Something big, and he wants rid of the crowd before he's found out."

"And theory two?"

"Someone else is up to no good in the mill and is leaning on Potts. That would mean that the someone else must have something on Potts.

"How did you suss that one?"

"A hunch."

"You and your hunches. You could be wrong, you know."

"Oh no. Hunches are good. They come from lots of little unconscious things we observe and then the brain processes it all. See?"

"I see. You've worked it all out, then."

"Well, actually it was a hunch and an overheard conversation, with a bit of luck thrown in. I happened to be in the right place at the right time."

"Do you want me to do anything about him?"

"No. There's a story there and I don't want him frightening off."

Ruth hung up and went into the main office.

"Has he surfaced yet?" Rocco asked.

"In a way, but not so that he's going to be of any help, Rocco. It's Saturday, there's an ocean of work to get through and I'm whacked."

"I have something that may or may not help. Julian's been on. Apparently the hessian sack the skeleton was found in had traces of cotton in it."

"Cotton? Do you mean pieces of cloth?" Ruth asked.

"No, I mean actual raw cotton, the fluffy stuff that comes in bales and is spun in the mills, or used to be. Julian says hessian is a relatively open mesh and that he found quite a quantity of cotton fibre embedded in it."

"That takes us back to Chase Mill. It was a cotton-spinning mill back in the day."

"Yes, but that was years ago."

"Cotton fibres can hang around, particularly in unused rooms," Imogen said.

"Did he say anything else?"

"Not yet. Doctor Barrington is doing the post-mortems on the two bodies. The one in the sack was relatively fresh. She'll do a report and get back to us."

"Good. Now we'll go and arrest Danny Newton. I have good information that he's living in the camp," Ruth said.

Rocco and Imogen exchanged glances. They'd be wondering who'd told her that, thought Ruth. She wrote 'cotton fibres' on the board next to the words 'sack' and 'locket.' "These are two different cases, aren't they? But we keep coming back to that mill. Snap and Ron lived in the homeless village and now the cotton fibres in the sacking the skeleton was found in. Plus the locket was found there. How can that be? What's the link and what's the motive? C'mon, guys — suggestions, bright ideas. Anyone got anything to add that'll help?"

"The girls could have run away. We know Lauren Steele did," Imogen said.

"No, she didn't, not really. She went to meet someone. Her mother reckons she'd never have left for good."

"She did go to the mill, we know that much. We have to ask what she was doing there and where did she go after that. We need a warrant to search that place."

Imogen was right. Ruth tapped her foot on the floor. "On balance I think we have enough to bring Danny Newton in. With a bit of luck he'll still be at the camp. Pass me the best photo you have of him. We'll take that with us for identity purposes. We'll bring him in, question him and hope that Macclesfield comes up with the goods to make it stick."

"Sergeant Bayliss! Could I have a word in my office?"

Ruth groaned inwardly. What did the DCI want? If it was more ear-bending about Calladine's disappearance, she'd scream!

Ruth went to the office. "I need a word anyway. We want to bring in someone from the homeless camp at the mill. We suspect he killed his partner."

"Get on with it, then. You know what to do."

"We also need a search warrant for the place. It is vital that we get inside. It's Saturday so I might need your help to get the warrant."

"I'll sort it. I have contacts."

The DCI gestured to a chair facing her across the desk. "Sit down. I appreciate how busy you are and I'm sorry to drag you away, but this is important. I was *not* responsible for having that house ransacked. I know how it must look to you and I don't blame you for being wary, but we have to trust each other."

This again. Ruth stared at the woman. She wanted to tell her that she didn't have to trust her at all, but she bit her tongue. The woman was the DCI after all.

Birch pushed some papers across the desk to Ruth. "Look at these. Pay particular attention to the amounts paid in."

They were copies of bank statements. Ruth couldn't see the name of the account holder; it was covered by Birch's hand. She scanned down the column the DCI was pointing to. There were monthly payments of his salary, but there were also other regular payments, amounting to thousands.

"Two or three thousand pounds each month for as long as I can go back. Stupid, don't you think, to put money earned that way into a standard current account where it can easily be found?" She tapped the papers.

"It depends how the money was earned."

"By being on Fallon's payroll, that's how. The payments came from an offshore account. People on the force who can find out about such things have confirmed that the money came from one of Fallon's accounts."

"Who does this account belong to?"

Birch did not respond.

"You are asking me to trust you. You have to give me something or we're back at square one. For all I know this could be your bank account."

"I wish it was. Look at the balance!"

"So — whose is it, then?"

"This must go no further. Very soon it will come out anyway, but until it does only me, you and Inspector Calladine can know."

Ruth nodded.

Birch pulled her hand away, revealing the name of the account holder.

Ruth was stunned.

* * *

Mirela was frantic. She'd walked carefully around each room on that floor, feeling at the panels nailed against the walls, but could find no way out. She presumed the panels covered the windows. Using the screwdriver she prised away splinters of wood, eventually making a small crack in one of them. It wasn't a window. It was a door and it was locked.

This was getting her nowhere and time was passing. She knew she hadn't hit Mac hard enough to kill him and he could wake up at any moment. Mirela banged against the wood with her fists but it was no use. She screamed. She'd never get out at this rate. Then a male voice spoke from behind her.

"This way, missy."

Mirela spun around. A tall man was beckoning to her.

"You want out, it's this way. Quick, before you're seen."

Mirela darted after him, clinging to the sleeve of his jacket. One steep staircase and several minutes later she was standing in the spring sunshine.

"You are an angel! I have been kept prisoner in there. I thought I would never get out and that he would kill me."

"We'd better shift or he'll be on our tails." He began pulling her along.

"I hit him. I hit him hard."

"But not hard enough, looking at the size of you. Come on, let's get you sorted."

"What's your name?"

"Call me Newt. And before you get too carried away I think that one good turn deserves another, don't you?"

"What do you mean?"

"I've done something for you, so now you can do something for me."

Mirela didn't like the look on his face. She'd just escaped from one hellhole and she had no intention of crashing headlong into another. If this bastard wanted to use her for his own ends, then he would be sorry. But for now all she could do was smile at him, to keep him sweet.

"Good girl. Come with me." He tugged her across a large open yard and through a gap in a wooden fence. "Not a word to anyone. Any questions, you say you're with me. Got it?"

"What day is it?"

"Saturday, that's why there's not many around. Most of them are off taking advantage of the generosity of

Leesdon's shoppers." Newt pulled her towards his tent, and Mirela hung back.

"Don't worry; it's not your body I want, sweet as it might be. I want you to help me play a joke on a pal of mine." Newt pushed her in front of him and placed his hand over her mouth.

Her mind was racing. What sort of joke? What friend? She didn't like the way this was going. She saw a woman washing pots a few yards away. This was the only chance she might get. This man wasn't going to help her. He was intent on some plan of his own. His hand was dirty and smelled foul. Mirela opened her mouth and bit down hard, until she tasted blood. Newt squealed and instantly released his grip on her.

Mirela ran towards the woman. Swearing, Newt ran back the way they'd come.

* * *

It was pointless chasing after her. She'd already got Cerys Powell's attention. Newt cursed his luck. He'd worked out what was going on and had decided to cut himself in. Mac was running girls from the mill, either on his own or with someone else. He reckoned Mac kept them there prior to moving them on. What to, he didn't know but he was sure it would be either prostitution or slavery. It was a lucrative business. Now it had all gone wrong. The girl would talk. She'd tell the police everything and he'd have a hell of a job getting out of it. He had to go away, but for that he needed money.

Newt ran back into the mill. Mac was still lying where she had hit him. He checked his pockets, looking for the keys to his vehicle and his wallet, but found nothing. He knew there must be a safe somewhere. With all the money to be made at this game, it had to contain a fortune. He picked up an old beer can, filled it with water from the shower and poured it over Mac's head.

Mac groaned.

"Keys — where are they?" Newt kicked him in the guts and pulled him up into a sitting position.

"Where did she go? Fucking bitch will get hers when I catch up with her."

"Don't waste your time, mate. She's long gone. She's probably telling the police all about it right now. You need to make plans and quick. A sure-fire exit out of here is what you need."

"Get me some water. I need to think."

"You need to do more than think, mate. You need to run. I don't think you understand the bother she can cause you. Me too, if I back up her story."

Mac lunged at him, but Newt easily dodged the blow. "If you're clever, you'll pay me off. You have money, must have. Where d'you stash it?"

"You're off your head."

"Yeah, you're right, and I've killed before too, so it won't take much to do for you."

Mac began to struggle to his feet. "I need to get out of here; she won't have gone far. She's got nowhere to go."

"You're not listening. I want money to get lost, and you'd be wise to do the same. You're not very good at this, are you? Lost one girl and couldn't find her, and now another's gone. I'd say you were a pretty shoddy operator. You need to sharpen up your act."

Mac grabbed Newt by the neck. "Leave it out, or I'll do you!"

"I don't think you will. In fact I think you should consider what I said. You and I should pool our resources."

"Get lost."

"The safe. Where is it? Pay me off and I'll go. I won't say a word about what I know."

Mac touched the back of his head. It was bleeding.

"I don't know who you are but you're pissing me off. Do one, before I smash your stupid face in."

Newt grinned at him. "Hear that? Sounds like police sirens to me."

Mac tried to stand but his legs wouldn't support him. Newt grabbed hold of his arms and dragged him across the floor.

"Get off me, you stupid bastard!"

"You are going to get me that money. Then I'll leave you alone." Newt lashed out, catching Mac on the chin and sending him reeling back to the floor. This wasn't getting him anywhere. He kicked at Mac's ribs and he howled. Newt was about to lay into him again when he felt a searing pain across his temple. His eyes opened wide and he span around. A man wearing a suit was standing behind him, wielding a crowbar. He hit him again across the side of his head and it all went black.

* * *

"Help me! I'm being chased. There's a man — I've been kept prisoner. They want to take me back to that room!"

Cerys took off her rubber gloves and ran across to the distraught girl. "It's okay. Whatever happened to you, you're safe now. We'll look after you."

"Mac! It was Mac and now that other one is chasing me. They made me do things . . . awful things, with men. You know what I mean."

Cerys Powell stared. Where had this girl come from? What she was saying sounded incredible. "Where were you kept?"

"Back there." Mirela pointed to the mill.

Working here Cerys thought she'd heard just about everything, but this was something else. The girl was shivering, and no wonder; she had hardly any clothes on. Cerys took a clean blanket from a shelf behind the counter and wrapped it around Mirela's shoulders.

"You're safe now. We'll look after you. We have someone here who is kind and gentle. She's called Stella

170

and she looks after the younger girls. I'll take you to meet her. She'll know what to do."

Cerys walked Mirela through the camp and caught up with Stella as she was leaving the shower block. Stella was a godsend. She'd taken on the role as camp 'mother', particularly where the young girls were concerned, runaways most of them and in a bad way by the time they found this place. She gave them a shoulder to cry on and a lot of sound advice, mostly to go home.

Cerys called out to her. "Have you got a moment?"

Mirela was sobbing. Stella walked towards them and looked at the girl. "Another one." She shook her head, looking at the girl more closely. "She's hardly dressed for living rough . . . I've seen her somewhere, I'm sure." She walked off towards her tent and returned with a photo in her hand. It showed Mirela with another girl who looked very like her.

Mirela snatched it from her. "Where did you get that? That is me! And the other girl is Anna, my sister."

"You'd better come with me." Stella moved aside and ushered her over to the tent. Cerys followed.

Inside the tent a girl was sitting on a quilt-covered mattress, brushing her long, dark hair. She looked at Mirela, gasped and held out her arms, screaming something in a language neither Stella nor Cerys could understand.

"They're sisters. Anna has been through hell. Her English is non-existent so I've no idea what happened, but she'd been badly beaten and half-starved by the time she got here."

Mirela turned to the women. "I came to England to find her. I used her computer and contacted her friends. One of them, a man, came from here. He said he'd help me. We became quite close online. I liked him. He sounded kind and he said he would help me to pay for accommodation while I looked for Anna. He gave me money. He even paid for my mother's medical treatment back home. For a while things were fine; he treated me like a lady. I thought he liked me . . ."

Her face crumpled and she brushed more tears from her cheeks.

". . . But then things changed. He said the money had been a loan not a gift and that he wanted it back. Each day the debt grew with the interest he added. I had no way of paying so he said I could work for him. Then he made me a prisoner in that place. He said Anna was there too. He used us both. Most nights he took me somewhere, a club I think. I was drugged and used by men who must have paid him a lot of money. He will have done the same with Anna. I will talk to her, find out what happened."

"She means the mill," Cerys told Stella. "She told me that's where she was being held."

"Do you know who by?"

"No — not yet." Cerys gestured for Stella to follow her outside. "Let's give them some time together before we do anything official."

At that moment they heard the police sirens.

Chapter 19

The police cars streamed past Calladine as he made his way back to the camp. He checked his mobile — nothing from Ruth. What the hell was going on?

A dark blue saloon pulled up beside him. Rocco was driving and Ruth sat in the passenger seat.

"Get in. We've got a warrant to search the mill. We're also going to arrest Danny Newton — Newt."

Calladine saw Rocco's face. "Yes, it's me, and no smart-arsed remarks, please. Has someone told Chase?"

"I didn't," said Ruth. "We wanted to keep the element of surprise."

"Surprise! The entire neighbourhood will know about it by now. You've made enough noise to wake the dead."

Ruth ignored this remark. "Two bodies were pulled out of the sewers yesterday. We're waiting on Doctor Barrington, but one was male, and I bet it's Ron or Snap. The other was wrapped in a hessian sack. The first sack with the skeleton in it had cotton fibres in the mesh."

"Everything keeps coming back to the mill."

"My thoughts exactly, and that's why we're going to have a damn good look inside."

"Newt will have heard the noise. You'll be lucky to catch him."

"If he has scarpered we'll organise the troops. Don't worry; we'll pick him up eventually."

"You've done very well. Doesn't look as if you've needed me at all."

"If I wasn't in this state, I'd tend to agree with you. The team have done a pretty good job, don't you think?"

"So what are we looking for at the mill?"

"First and foremost, Danny Newton — this Newt person. Then anything that proves the girl or girls were kept there."

The car pulled into the mill car park. As he got out Calladine was already peeling off the false facial hair and teasing the wig from his scalp.

Ruth chuckled. "You look even worse now. The glue has left marks on your face."

"Why were you undercover anyway, sir? Because of the case?"

"No, Rocco. It was a personal matter. I didn't think anyone would think to look for me here."

Cerys stood waiting for them.

"Is the security guard here?" Ruth asked.

Cerys shook her head and stared at him.

"We have a warrant to search the place. Have you seen Newt?"

"Not since breakfast. You were living here . . . but . . . you're the detective?"

"Yes, but don't worry. It had nothing to do with what you're doing."

"Uniform are in, sir," said Rocco. "They've knocked through the fence and the rear doors."

Cerys looked frightened. "Mr Chase won't be happy. He'll blame us. He'll be keener than ever to move us out now. He'll have the bailiffs back before we can draw breath."

She had a point. Calladine looked around. These people couldn't stay here forever, but they had nowhere else to go.

"A girl turned up this morning. She said she'd been kept prisoner in the mill. She's Anna's sister. Anna's the girl staying with Stella. She's had a bad time of it too. Whoever imprisoned her was a very evil man."

"What do you mean, Cerys?"

"She said he used her — got men to pay money to . . . you know."

"Someone was using these girls for prostitution? And keeping them in there?"

Cerys nodded.

"Where's Eddie Potts?"

"My Eddie wouldn't have anything to do with this! He's not like that."

Calladine raised his eyebrows. The young woman had no idea. "Where is he?"

"He's cleaning the showers."

Calladine nodded at one of the uniformed officers. "Go and get him. Take him down to the station. You can't miss him; he's got bright red hair."

"Ground, first and second floors all clear, sir!" Rocco was following the uniformed officers round the mill and Calladine ran over to catch them up.

"I'm looking for somewhere girls could have been kept."

"I thought we were looking for Danny Newton."

"C'mon, let's go round again. Start in the basement."

They climbed down the stairs. Peering through the door Calladine could see that the entire underground space was given over to storage, with a shower block at one end. It was built from stone, and was icy cold. Calladine shivered.

A male voice called out to them from the corner of the room.

"My security man has been attacked! The madman came at him with that thing." He pointed to a crowbar lying on the floor. "They both need to go to hospital. I'm afraid I had to intervene. He fell. You might like to check how he is."

It was Damien Chase. Calladine went across to look at the man lying on the floor. He hadn't seen him in the dark room. It was Newt. Calladine checked him over. "This man's dead. How hard did you hit him?"

At that moment Mac appeared from one of the showers. He staggered towards them, clutching his belly. "The bastard flew at me. If Mr Chase hadn't turned up, I'd be the one lying down there, an iron bar in my skull."

"You're Childers, the security man."

He nodded. "I only asked him to leave. This place is dangerous if you don't know the layout. He flipped. Came at me swearing his head off and brandishing that thing."

"Did you see this happen, Mr Chase?"

"Not exactly. I arrived just in time to save the day."

"Get a forensic team down here, Rocco. Did you see the girl?"

Mac Childers looked at Calladine, then at Chase. "What girl?"

"The one that was being held here."

"Who told you that fairy tale, Inspector? It is the inspector, isn't it? Only you look a little different from when we met the last time."

"You'll need to give a statement, Mr Childers. You too, Mr Chase."

"My head needs looking at," muttered Mac.

"I'll have one of my officers take you to A & E and then down to the station."

"I can take him and then bring him over, Inspector," said Chase.

"No — not on your own. You'll go with a uniformed officer. A man has been killed here."

* * *

"I want the Duggan to take Newt's body. I want to know exactly what happened to him."

Calladine's mobile rang. It was Ruth.

"Imogen's been on. She has a possible identity for the skeleton. A girl called Tracy Draper has been missing from Huddersfield for two years. She had the right medical history, her dental records are a close match and she was on the transplant list. Julian has already started the DNA extraction from the bones and the hospital has all her details on record. That means we should get a positive match fairly soon. Then we can contact her family."

"Good work. Anything else?"

"Not for now. Have you got Danny Newton in custody?"

"He was involved in a fight with Childers, the security bloke. He's dead, I'm afraid. Childers is on his way to A&E with an escort."

Rocco called out. "They've found something, sir!"

"I'll have to go, Ruth. I'll meet you outside. In the meantime, have a word with the girl Cerys found. She reckons she was kept prisoner in here."

Rocco led the way up to the fifth floor and into a small room off the right-hand side of the corridor. It was dark inside and the window had been boarded up. In one corner was a blanket, a small candle and a half-finished bottle of water. "It looks like this was where one of them was kept, sir. There are other similar rooms along here, all with nothing but a blanket and a candle. So that means the girl that turned up today wasn't the only one."

Calladine walked around the small space. Poor girl, whoever she was. She must have spent hours in this cold room, in fear and with no one to talk to.

Were these the girls put in sacks and dumped in the sewer system?

"We need to speak to that girl. Find out what she knows about this operation."

"This can't be down to Newt — Danny Newton," said Rocco. "He's not been here long enough. He was living near Macclesfield just a few months ago."

"I think you're right, Rocco. But Newt found out somehow and I'll lay odds he wanted in. So the question remains, who was running the show?"

"That bloke, Mac Childers?" Rocco suggested.

* * *

"Her name is Mirela Popescu. She's Romanian. She has no idea how long she's been here but Mac definitely used her for prostitution. He took her to clubs. He always took her in his van, and she says sometimes the journey was short, other times it was longer. Mirela reckons she was always drugged. And the bastard used to beat her. Tonight she was supposed to entertaining a friend of Mac's — a special friend is how Mac described him. It was when he took her for a shower to get her ready that she managed to escape. On one occasion recently she did see someone else, well heard him really; he kept in the shadows. She got the impression that Mac was working for him."

"Will she speak to me, Ruth?"

"I doubt it, Tom. She's in the tent with her sister, Anna. Mirela came here to find Anna. Mac groomed them both online. He promised them money and a good life. That didn't last long. He quickly brought her here and said the money he'd already given her was a loan and accruing interest daily."

"Debt slavery. Did she try to get away?"

"She's a delicate little thing and he beat her. He kept her locked up and he drugged her so she couldn't fight the customers off. There was no way she could get out of that."

"This other man — any ideas?"

"She can't describe him. Anna doesn't speak English but Mirela asked her about him and she'd no idea. Anna only ever saw Mac. But Anna does remember there being other girls here. They cried out during the day and screamed whenever they were taken away. She says that during the last few weeks things got quieter. I reckon that's because of the homeless village. They'll have had to curtail the operation somewhat."

"We'll need a statement off them both. They can't stay here. A check-up at the hospital, then a safe place until we have the full story. They must be guarded at all times. Mac and Chase have gone to A&E. Newt clobbered Mac and paid for it with his life."

"I think Lauren Steele fell into their clutches too. And if she did, where is she now? In fact, where are the rest of the girls? What's happened to them?"

"We need to speak to Mac Childers."

"He'll deny it all. What proof do we have?"

"We have Mirela's testimony. He kept her prisoner. I've had Newt's body taken to the Duggan. We might get something from that."

"Newt lived here. We should search his tent."

Ruth passed him a pair of gloves and a handful of evidence bags.

"I'll get on with it. You get transport organised to take the girls to the hospital. You'd better ask Stella if she'll go with them."

Calladine walked across the yard to Newt's tent. It looked as if a bomb had hit it. There were empty beer cans and cigarette butts all over the floor and flies were buzzing around a half-eaten sandwich festering on top of a box. The inspector snapped on a pair of gloves and started to move things around. There wasn't much. No documents and no identification. But in a coat pocket he found a photo of Newt with a woman. He placed it in an evidence bag. Somewhat reluctantly, he got down on the floor to look under the mattress. Amidst more rubbish, tucked in right at the back, lay a machete.

Chapter 20

Calladine went back to his house for a shower and a change of clothes. The uniformed officer was still there and looked surprised to see him.

"I do live here, Constable."

His house was much as he'd left it. Being here again reminded him that he was still in danger. So much was going on in the job he'd pushed the Fallon thing to the back of his mind. One way or another, he had to get this case sorted.

Fifteen minutes later he looked like his old self, dressed in a clean shirt and his grey suit. A quick mug of coffee and he'd be off back to the nick.

But Rhona Birch was letting herself into his house. "I told you to keep in touch! Anything could have happened to you. That would have meant your neck and my job, DI Calladine."

"I had things to do. The case, it won't solve itself. We've got two dead men and a racket in trafficked girls to sort. What do you expect from me?"

"I expect you to obey orders. You are no good to anyone dead."

"Get yourself a coffee if you want." As she walked through, he pocketed his wallet and phone.

"You don't trust me, that much is obvious. But you should. I might be all that stands between you and a bullet."

"That's rich. I tell you I'll stay at my mother's house and within the hour it's done over. What if I'd really been there?"

"You never had any intention, did you? You set me up."

"Well, it worked."

Birch lowered her heavy frame into one of his armchairs. "I did tell someone else. I told the chief super."

"Edwin Walker? Are you suggesting that *he* had the house trashed?"

"Yes, I am. He's on the take. He receives thousands each month from an offshore bank account belonging to Fallon."

Calladine stared at the woman. No, she definitely wasn't joking. "I take it you have proof?"

"Naturally. What do you take me for? You should also know that it was him that came up with that wild theory about you planting evidence. He wanted you on leave, isolated from your colleagues, to make the job easier for Fallon's hitman."

"So what's next? What do we do?"

"We do nothing except keep our mouths shut. He'll be dealt with, quietly and swiftly, before Fallon puts a bullet through his head."

"Eve will be devastated."

"Not our problem."

His phone rang. Rocco.

"Both Chase and Childers are back from A&E. Chase is kicking off. We've separated them both. We've put them in separate soft interview rooms and given them a hot drink. Chase has rung his solicitor and will walk if we don't get on with things."

"Okay, Rocco. I'm coming in." He turned to Birch.

"I need to go to the nick. Damien Chase, the mill owner, is waiting to be interviewed. He killed a man tonight and I'm not entirely sure why. He reckoned he was protecting his security man but I don't trust him. I've got three suspects in the frame for this: Mac Childers, Eddie Potts and now Damien Chase. One of them is the main player behind the prostitution ring. All I have to do now is work out which one."

"Can't the girls identify him?"

"The two we've rescued didn't see him. If Childers isn't the main man, he might talk if we offer him a deal."

"We can't promise him anything. And you need to be in witness protection."

"Ma'am, if you're going to keep sticking that old record on we'll get nowhere."

She shrugged and checked her watch. "Work inside the station and don't leave it. That's the best I can do."

"Okay."

* * *

"Julian is rushing the tests through, sir," said Imogen. "He reckons there's blood on the machete blade so he'll see if it matches either Snap or Ron's."

"Ron's body hasn't turned up yet. It must still be down the sewer. We need to look at the map again. We're looking for access somewhere near to Chase Mill."

"I'll contact the water people again. They've been very helpful so far. Good to see you back, sir. Hope things are okay."

"So do I, Imogen. For the time being I'm grounded. Not allowed out of the building I'm afraid. You and Rocco did a good job finding out about Newton — well done, both of you."

Ruth looked up from her desk. "So what are we short of?"

"Proof. The girl, Mirela, can identify Mac Childers but we have nothing positive to link Potts or Chase to any of this. I want to know as much as possible about those two men and quick. You can speak to Cerys Powell about Potts, find out about his movements over the last week or so. The pair live together. But how do we find out about Chase? The minute he suspects we're ferreting about in his private life he'll have his lawyers at our throats."

"We know he owns clubs, sir. One of them is on Oldston High Street. We could visit. See what goes on."

"That will take too long. Those places don't open until late and they stay open until the early hours. Anyway the minute we're spotted, anything dodgy would be covered up."

"I'll get the CCTV then. That should give us a good idea of who uses the place. According to the accounts they aren't doing too well so it shouldn't take long."

"Good idea. I'll leave that one with you."

"All this is very frustrating. Mac Childers knows the truth. Could we broker a deal?" Rocco asked.

"We can try. We'll make that the first onslaught."

"Do you know who sent you the camera?" Ruth asked. "Because whoever did must have realised its importance."

"I've no idea, and I've really had no time to think about it."

"It must have been someone in the camp."

Ruth was right. But Calladine had no idea who.

"I'll speak to Childers first. Rocco, do you want in on this?"

Calladine had decided not to involve Ruth in case things got heated. She'd had enough stress this week. He and Rocco left the office and strode off down the corridor. "I intend to make it plain what he's facing. If he still won't play ball, then we'll throw the book at him."

Childers was sitting in one of the soft interview rooms, sipping coffee.

"You took your time. Can I go now? The hospital said I might have concussion and I should rest."

Calladine smiled at him. "You can get off soon. But we're a little curious about the mill, and what went on there."

"Nothing went on; it's empty. Once that rabble have gone, the place will be sold and demolished. Good riddance, that's what I say."

"Explain to me about Danny Newton. What were the two of you arguing about?"

"He was trespassing. I told him to get lost. When he refused I went to throw him out and he attacked me."

"And Mr Chase came to your rescue?"

"I think so," he rubbed his head. "That's right, he must have done. He pulled him off me but Newton wouldn't stop."

"So Chase hit him?"

"I suppose he must have. I didn't see, I'd been clobbered myself."

Tell me about the girls."

"What girls?"

"Come on, Mr Childers. We know that girls were held prisoner there. We talked to one of them and in time we'll talk to a second one. We found the rooms. The evidence is mounting. We will find your DNA in those rooms. We'll find men who will tell us about the girls to save their own skin. They'll tell us it was all arranged through you. There is no escape from this, Mr Childers. If you talk to us it might go better for you when this goes to court."

"You're bluffing! You have nothing on me. I've got nowt to say. I'm leaving." Childers began to get to his feet.

"We have two girls who will identify you. They will testify that you beat them and hired them out for the purpose of prostitution."

"They're lying. They might say things, but you still can't prove it. I'm out of here."

184

"I'm afraid you're not, Mr Childers, because I'm going to arrest you for the unlawful imprisonment of Anna and Mirela Popescu."

"You can't do that. I don't even know them. I just work there. I walk around twice a day and check the gates. That's not against the law, is it?"

Calladine nodded at the uniformed officer. "Take him to the cells."

"What now?" said Rocco.

"We'll have to talk to Chase. I'd like to know why he felt the need to hit Newt so hard it killed him."

* * *

"You've wasted enough of my time already, Inspector. Whatever you want, get on with it. I have a business to run."

"I'm afraid it's not that simple, Mr Chase. A man was killed in your mill today, by you."

"I've explained that. He was attacking my security man. If I hadn't intervened, he'd have killed him."

"What I don't understand is why you had to hit Danny Newton so hard? And unfortunately Mr Childers is still a tad confused about exactly what did happen."

"Ask him again," he said with frustration. "Childers must realise I saved his life."

"What do you know about the prostitution racket being run from your mill."

"Inspector! If that is true, and I doubt very much that it is you can't seriously believe I'd be mixed up in anything like that?"

"We have the evidence. We have the girls. It's only a matter of time before we have enough to pin this where it belongs."

"Well, it certainly won't be pinned on me, Inspector. I'm a businessman. I operate a number of legitimate operations. Your time would be better spent looking among the down and outs who've been camped at the mill and blighting my life all these weeks. It's staring you in the face. What sort of detective are you?" Chase got to his feet. "So unless you have something positive, something concrete proving I committed a crime, don't bother me with this anymore."

He walked to the door.

"I'm very sorry, Mr Chase. But you are going to have to stay with us a little longer. I'm not entirely satisfied with what the pair of you have told me about Newton's death. We will need to speak to you again."

"Inspector, I'm going home. I can be trusted. I have no intention of fleeing the country. You are barking up the wrong tree. I have done nothing wrong."

"That isn't how it works. For the time being you will be kept in the cells. Also we will require a DNA sample and your fingerprints."

"I don't like him; he's a slimy bastard," Rocco said, once Chase had left the room.

"I agree, but that alone doesn't make him guilty of all this."

* * *

Calladine got straight to the point. "Julian, I need to find the man behind all this, and I need solid proof. I can get Childers on some of it, but he was just doing as he was told. He was the brawn, not the brains, but he's being stubborn."

"We are working as hard as we can, Inspector. Doctor Barrington is doing the post-mortem on the bodies. We have a positive ID on Snap Langton, and on Newton. His DNA is on file. The other body, the young girl, we are still checking. Ruth suggested it might be Lauren Steele. Her mother's DNA is on file; it was taken when she went missing, so we are doing the checks. There is something else, however. She was put into two different sacks; one that covered the lower part of her body and another over the upper half. This offered a degree of protection from

186

predators and the effects of water. Doctor Barrington tells me that it looks as if she had a fight before she died. There is evidence of bruising about the face and two teeth are missing. But, most interesting of all, she still has tissue wedged under her fingernails. She fought back, and scratched her assailant. We should be able to get DNA from that and with luck match it to her killer. There is no water in her lungs so she was dead before she was put into the sewer. A sharp blow to the head, the doctor tells me."

"Thanks, Julian. I'd come over but I'm grounded for the time being."

"I will phone later with an update."

Chapter 21

Imogen popped her head around his office door. "Eddie Potts is waiting to be interviewed. He's got Cerys Powell with him. And there's a woman downstairs asking to see you, guv. Do I send her up first?"

"Do we have a name?"

"Marilyn. That's all she'd say."

Calladine only knew one Marilyn, and that was Ray Fallon's wife. He should say no. Although she had called him and tried to warn him about the danger he was in, she could still be here to do him harm and he didn't trust her. She wasn't a bad woman herself, but she'd always stuck by Fallon, somehow managing to turn a blind eye to all his villainy.

Against his better judgement he said, "I'll see her."

His stomach churned. Well, this was a police station after all.

She smiled tentatively as she came through the door. "I wasn't sure if you'd want to see me. I know what's going on; Ray's been boasting about it. He does nothing but shout his head off. He tells anyone who'll listen how he's striking down the witnesses one by one. He's certain there'll be no one left to testify against him when the time comes."

"I know what he's up to. He had Lydia killed." He studied the woman who stood before him. "Did you know what he was going to do, then? Could you have stopped it?"

She shook her head vigorously. "But perhaps I should have realised. I ought to know him by now — and how he operates. I should hate him for it, for everything he's done but I can't. He's still my husband, Tom and I still love him."

Calladine couldn't imagine anyone loving Fallon. "You met her once," he said.

"Yes, I know. She was the pretty, blonde girl who came house-hunting on our road. We talked about dogs. I liked her . . . You must be wondering why I'm here. To be honest, I'm wondering myself. I want to do something. I want to try and put some of this right, but it would mean betraying Ray and I don't think I can do that."

"He's killing people, Marilyn. Lydia is dead and he's after me. God knows who he'll target next."

"Just coming to see you, talking about this, has taken some doing, believe me. I know what Ray is. He's a cold, murdering bastard. I don't know how I've stood it for so long."

There were tears in her eyes. This was a very different Marilyn from the one he knew. She flopped down in the chair on the other side of his desk. She looked a mess. Marilyn usually carried her fifty-eight years extremely well, but not today. She wasn't wearing make-up and her face looked gaunt and heavily lined. There were dark circles beneath her eyes.

"I'm sorry about your mum, Tom. I wanted to come to the funeral but Ray wouldn't let me. I wish now that I'd insisted. I liked your mum. She was kind to me when I first married Ray. I didn't appreciate it back then, but she gave me some very good advice."

"What did she tell you?"

"She told me to ditch him. She said Ray was no good and that he'd bring me down. She was right. I've never been so unhappy. I doubt I'll make it through this."

"Wise woman, Freda. You'll be alright, Marilyn. We just need to make sure the bastard goes down this time."

"But he won't, will he? Not if we leave it up to the law. You know as well as I do that the law doesn't always get it right. Where Ray's concerned, it's never got it right. I came to warn you, to make you understand how serious this is. I know he wants you dead. He's got a contract out on your head. He doesn't mess up where things like this are concerned, Tom. He's got money and he gets the best. I've tried to talk some sense into him but he won't listen. I'm here to warn you. To tell you to take all the protection you'll be offered. The police can hide you away until the trial."

She went quiet, and stared down at her hands. Calladine noticed she'd taken her wedding ring off. "I can't do that, Marilyn. I've got work to do. A big case to wind up."

"You, and a lot of good people will suffer if he gets off. He'll never stop. He'll rob and cheat and kill until the day he dies."

"I can't hide away. If I testify then the chances are he'll go down for a very long time."

"He'll never stand it. Prison for any length of time will drive him insane. He's already showing the signs."

"So what are you suggesting?"

"I don't know. If it comes to a choice, I don't want him back on the streets but I don't want him to suffer either."

"You've got me stumped, Marilyn."

"I know things. I know about bank accounts, people on his payroll, people who feed him information . . . but most important, I know who he gets to do his dirty work. I know who he gets to carry out the killings."

If what she was telling him was true, her information could finish Fallon for good. "This is huge, Marilyn. Are you prepared to speak to the police about this? Perhaps give evidence in court — face him in the dock. Could you do that?"

"No, never, and that's the problem. I came to warn you but I'm not ready to shop him. I'd hate myself and I couldn't stand for him to know that it was me."

"Ray won't be happy that you came at all."

"He won't find out," she smiled. "Because if he thought for one moment that I had spoken to you he might even put a price on *my* head."

She was probably right. Calladine could hardly believe that Marilyn had come to him like this. She had always turned a blind eye, played the dizzy blonde and let Ray Fallon get away with murder, literally.

* * *

He returned to the main office.

"Is that who I think it is?" Ruth asked.

"Yep. She came to warn me. I think she's close to spilling her guts. If she does, then Fallon is really done for this time. She could hand over names, dates, bank details, everything we need in fact."

"Did Birch tell you about Edwin Walker?"

"Yes, she did. I'm still not sure whether to believe her or not."

"She told me too. I wouldn't take her word for it that she didn't set you up, so she showed me some bank statements. They were Walker's. His name was on them and the amounts paid in were regular and large. I would have told you before but events at the mill made things a bit hectic."

Imogen interrupted their conversation. "I've done some research on Damien Chase. We know he owns three night clubs. According to the latest accounts all of them are failing. So why does he keep them going?"

"Good question, Imogen." Calladine sat down on the edge of Joyce's desk to listen to her.

"I looked at the CCTV from Oldston High Street. There is a camera directly opposite one of Chase's clubs. The place is heaving most nights, despite what the accounts say. And — this is the interesting bit — the clientele are almost all men. Hardly any women go there."

"So on paper there's not much money coming in, but CCTV tells us a different story."

"It certainly does. He charges a substantial entry fee too. You can see people handing over hefty sums on the door."

"So what's the attraction?"

Ruth and Imogen looked at each other.

"Tell him," Ruth urged.

"We've all been on this — Joyce, Rocco and me. We've been through the CCTV from last week: Friday and Saturday night. Last Friday night, Eddie Potts visited. We should have a word with him and get him to tell us what he was doing there."

Imogen looked again at Ruth. "Tell him what we think."

"Chase is using his clubs as knocking shops; that's what the girls are for. But that's not all of it — he's selling them too . . ."

The office phone rang. Joyce held it out to him. "Julian wants you."

"Got anything yet?"

"We've no match for the tissue found under the girl's fingernails. Get me a sample from one of your suspects and then we'll see."

That was a blow. "Okay, Julian. I'll see what I can get this end. There was a locket too. It belonged to Lauren Steele, identified by her sister. Would you test it for fingerprints? We might get lucky but if we don't we've still a couple of suspects lined up."

"I'll get it sorted, Inspector."

Calladine turned back to the team. "Who's looking after Mirela and her sister? I don't want them disappearing."

"WPC Kate Robinson," said Rocco. "She's good. You might remember her from the 'Vida' case. She worked as family liaison."

"Do you think she can persuade Mirela to talk to us? At least give a statement, perhaps look at some photos and pick out Childers."

"I'm sure she can. I'll speak to her."

"Keep me posted, will you?"

"Inspector Calladine!"

It was DCI Birch.

"Come to my office, please."

She sounded almost friendly. She passed him some papers.

"Edwin Walker's bank statements, and I owe you an apology. Like I told you at your house it was me who told him you were going to your mother's. If you'd actually been there, I could have been responsible for getting you killed."

"Well, that's cleared that up. I also deliberately misled you. I'm not sure why, instinct I suppose."

"You and I will have to learn to trust one another, Inspector." And she smiled at him.

* * *

"You were caught on CCTV going into Chase's club in Oldston last weekend. What were you doing there?"

Eddie shrugged. "Clubbing, drinking, having a little boogie with the girls."

"What girls?"

"Cerys and some friends."

"Cerys wasn't there. The clientele was monitored going in and out and there were precious few women in the club that night or any other. So come on, Eddie. What really goes on in there?"

193

"Look, Inspector, I've done nowt. Childers said it was a good place to go. He said if I went I could get some good gear — you know."

"Drugs?" asked Rocco.

"I'm not saying any more. Why should I? I'll only incriminate myself."

"We're not interested in your petty drug dealing, Potts. Just answer the question," said Calladine.

"I sell a bit of dope around the camp, but it can be hard to get hold of. Childers said that if I went to the club he could get me some. So I went."

"What was going on there, Eddie?"

"Nothing. I saw nothing."

"Keep this up and you're going to be charged with a very serious offence. I'm not talking dope either. I'm talking murder, Eddie. Do you want that? How do you think Cerys will feel about you, then?"

"You can't tell her I was at that club; she'll kill me. She doesn't know about the dope either."

"Then talk to me, lad."

There was a silence. Calladine watched as Eddie shuffled uncomfortably on his seat. Finally he spoke.

"There are girls there, dozens of them. You can buy sex; it's cheap and plentiful. Childers saw me kissing a girl. He said he'd tell Cerys and then he said he'd keep quiet if I helped him get rid of the camp."

"That's why you sent the bones?"

"I knew about the rats in Stockport. It worked there; that camp broke up. So I thought the bones might work here, scare them off."

"What else was going on at the club, Eddie?"

"There was a special room. A lot of blokes — well-dressed blokes — were bidding for the girls. It sounded like some sort of auction. I watched for a bit with Childers. The girls were selling for thousands. They were selling on the internet, too. The whole operation must be worth a small fortune."

"Get his statement, Rocco. Make sure he doesn't miss any little detail out. Get his fingerprints, as well as a DNA sample."

"Look, Inspector, none of this is down to me. I did try to help. It was me who sent you that camera. I thought the photos on it might be important."

Chapter 22

"What do you think?"

"Did you watch, Ruth?"

"Yes, and for what it's worth I think he's telling the truth. The bit about the camera swung it for me."

"I've had enough of pussyfooting around. Get Childers to an interview room and come with me," he said to Imogen."

This was it. Whether Childers talked or not, he had enough now to search Chase's clubs.

As they went, Calladine took a detour into Birch's office. "I want to raid Chase's club in Oldston. He's running a racket in girls from there. I want evidence gathering before it disappears. I'm about to interview another suspect, so would you organise it?"

"Certainly, Inspector. Leave it to me."

"Make sure you get all the IT equipment too," he added.

"You and her getting along a bit better, guv?"

"We have no choice."

Childers looked up as they entered and smiled.

"I know about the clubs and what goes on there. I'm about to formally arrest your partner, Chase. Now, do you think he'll be shy about dropping you in it?"

The smile vanished.

"I want a lawyer," he said at last.

Calladine nodded at the uniformed officer by the door.

"If you talk it will help you later, but you don't have long. Tell me your side of the story now before Chase has the chance to drop you in it. If you don't, then you'll be facing a murder charge."

"I ain't killed no one. I wouldn't. I told him I drew the line at that. So he had to do it. It irritated the hell out of him but I didn't give a stuff."

"Who are we talking about, Mac? Say his name for the tape."

"Damien Chase. He did the killings, all of them. I just got rid of the bodies."

"What goes on in those clubs of his?"

"Knocking shops is what they are. He gets me to find the girls online and tempt them in. Poor little rich bloke has to make his money any way he can."

"But there's more to it than that."

"He sells them. He buys and then resells at a profit. They go all over the world."

"What did you do with the bodies, Mac?"

"I wrapped them up in sacks and put them down the manhole. Chase said it led directly into the sewer . . . The first one was the worst. She was ill and couldn't hack the pace. She collapsed in the club one night so Chase clobbered her."

"Tracy?"

"Yeah, how do you know?"

"Like I said, we've been gathering evidence. How many more did he kill?"

"A couple more and then there was the blonde girl. She was lippy, always arguing. One night in the club she didn't take the drugs, just pretended. She started telling the punters what was going on. She had everyone shit-scared. Customers were leaving and some didn't come back. Chase said she had to go."

"What was her name?"

"Lauren."

Calladine wanted to hit him then. Lauren Steele. The recording of the interview would be a chilling listen. Childers talked about the young women as if they somehow deserved to be killed. And as for getting rid of the bodies — he seemed to see it as just another part of the job.

"Get his DNA and fingerprints. Then get his statement on paper."

* * *

"Chase is in the cells shouting his head off about a travesty of justice and suing the arse off the force," said Rocco.

"His clubs are being raided. His IT equipment should prove interesting." Calladine picked up the phone.

"Julian, I'm having Chase's computers sent over. We're looking for anything that links him to slavery, trading girls online, grooming, people trafficking, you know the sort of stuff."

"I'll have a look and then I'll send the lot on to IT forensics but they are not in until Monday now. Incidentally there are other prints on that locket, Inspector, apart from Lauren's. We have no match on record so that eliminates both Potts and Childers."

"Thanks, Julian. Chase's DNA and prints should be with you soon."

"It'll be pushing it to process both today, but I will look at his prints."

"With Childers's statement, we have enough to charge Chase and hold him. The only problem will be the fancy lawyer he might have up his sleeve. Thanks, Julian. See you later."

He looked around at the team. "Right, who wants in on this one?"

"I'd like to join you, sir," said Rocco.

Imogen had her eyes fixed on her computer screen and Ruth was yawning her head off. Rocco it was.

* * *

Uniform brought Damien Chase in. He'd been shouting the odds all the way down the corridor and had his brief in tow.

"Remember, he's slippery. He'll do everything he can to wriggle out of this," said Calladine.

In the interview room Chase was sitting alongside his brief, who was shuffling papers.

The lawyer spoke first. "This is harassment, Inspector."

"This is Raymond Hughes, my solicitor. Now, let's get this nonsense sorted so that I can leave here as soon as possible."

"Tell me what goes on in those clubs of yours, Mr Chase."

"The usual things: drinking, dancing, young people getting together, getting to know one another . . ."

"A lot more than that goes on though, doesn't it? Tell me about the girls. Tell me about the sex, the auctions. Tell me about trading girls over the internet."

"The man's lost his head! Where has all this nonsense sprung from?"

"Mac Childers has given us a full statement. As has Eddie Potts who visited your club in Oldston and saw for himself what goes on there."

"In that case I'd ask them to explain these fairy tales. I have no idea what they or you are talking about, Inspector. None of this makes any sense or has anything to do with me."

Chase whispered something in Hughes's ear.

"My client wants to leave now," said the solicitor.

"I'll bet he does. But that's not going to happen. You're staying with us for a while, Mr Chase. We're searching your clubs and we'll examine your IT equipment. Whatever you are trying to hide, we will find it. It is my intention to charge you with the murders of at least two young women. After we've finished our searches, the number will possibly increase. Plus the false imprisonment of many more."

Chase looked directly back at Calladine. There was no flicker of doubt or uncertainty in his bland expression. "Nonsense, all of it."

"What evidence do you have currently, Inspector?" asked Hughes.

"Statements from two others who are directly involved."

"Someone else's word against that of my client?"

Calladine nodded.

"These girls you found — can they identify my client directly?"

"No, they never saw him."

"In that case you must arrest my client or let him go. If you arrest him we will apply for bail."

Minutes later, Calladine had read Chase his rights and arrested him. Now all they could do was wait for forensics to come up with the goods.

Hughes placed a reassuring hand on Chase's shoulder. "I will get bail organised."

"In the meantime you will return to the cells," said Calladine.

"If I refuse?"

"You have no choice. I'm afraid it's me calling the shots now."

* * *

Imogen wore a look of great satisfaction. "Sir, there is a large manhole at the back of Chase Mill and it leads directly into the main sewer tunnel. First thing tomorrow the water board will put the robot down and have a look."

"With any luck they'll find Ron."

"Do you think there are any other girls down there?"

"It's possible. Childers mentioned another two and for all we know Chase could have been at this for years."

"So where do Snap and Ron fit into all this?" Ruth asked.

"Danny Newton. Newt came to the camp looking for Snap and killed him. As we know, Snap had witnessed Newt burying Grace Bracewell. He couldn't risk that getting out. I think that one night Newt saw what Childers was up to, possibly when Childers disposed of Lauren's body. Newt decided to use the manhole himself. As far as he was concerned it was a perfect place to dispose of bodies. He was scared that Snap had talked to his mate, Ron. So he killed him too, just to make sure."

"Sounds plausible."

"We'll never really know, because Newt can't tell us now. All we're waiting for is the Duggan to give us the absolute proof that Chase is our man. But we won't have that today." He looked round the office. It was late Saturday afternoon and they were all still hard at it. "Listen up, folks. I know we said we'd meet up tonight in the Wheatsheaf, but would you mind if we did it tomorrow lunchtime instead?"

"That suits me," said Ruth. "I really haven't got the energy today."

"And I'd rather crack on with this," said Imogen, looking up from her computer.

"Okay. Imogen, tell Julian and get him to pass the message on to Tash Barrington. I'll ring the doc."

Chapter 23

It was the same routine every time Marilyn visited the damn place. She had to leave her handbag and coat in a locker and then they searched her. A female warden clapped her palms up and down her body, making her feel sick and tense. Finally, when they were satisfied she wasn't trying to smuggle in a weapon, drugs or anything else, she was allowed through. The only consolation for Marilyn was that this would be the last time.

He was seated alone at a table, waiting for her. He looked harmless enough. He was clean-shaven and his dark hair was cut short — it suited him actually. He smiled as she approached. If they'd led a different life, if he'd been a different sort of man, they could have been happy. Maybe they even would have had children.

"Couldn't bring anything, babe. They wouldn't have let me in if I had."

"Bloody screws. I'll sort them when I get out."

More hate. Where did it all come from, Marilyn wondered. "The way things are going, you won't be getting out. They're building a pretty strong case, Ray."

"I'm working through a list. Next on it is that interfering cousin of mine. Once he's out of the way

202

there'll be no case to answer. No witnesses, you see!" He threw his arms in the air.

"I don't like it. You're taking risks. This isn't some movie, you know."

"I've got no choice. Thomas takes the stand and I'm going down for a long time, Marilyn. You don't want that, do you?"

"You look pale. Have you been taking your pills?"

"I'm bloody rattling."

"Do you need something now? Your colour's not right."

"Tell the screw — he'll get them."

Marilyn went across to the guard.

"He's bringing something. That was a big heart operation, Ray. You need to be careful. Taking your pills regularly is important."

The guard returned and put two tablets in Ray Fallon's palm.

"I'll get you some water." Marilyn got to her feet and walked to a sink in the far corner of the room.

She took a plastic beaker from a dispenser and turned on the water tap. She let it run, ensuring it was cold. While she waited she was twisting a hollow, gold bangle on her wrist, round and around. It looked like an unconscious act, a habit. But it wasn't. Marilyn was releasing something into the beaker — a clear liquid, hidden inside the hollow bracelet.

"Pills in your mouth. Now drink this and swallow the lot down."

Ray Fallon smiled; she was mothering him again. He opened his mouth and did as he was told.

"I'm sorry, Ray. I wish things could have been different, I really do. I loved you once, in some ways I still do. You were my world."

He grinned at her. "Soft tart."

"Don't talk. We don't have long and I want you to know what I've done. I had to, you gave me no choice.

You might be in prison but you're out of control. You are so full of hate I don't know who you are anymore. If you got off again, I couldn't take you back, not now. If you get sent down, I know how much you'd suffer. I had to do something. This is it Ray, this is goodbye." She kissed his cheek.

Ray looked confused, he thought she was just talking the sentimental crap that women always talked.

Marilyn bit her lip as she waited and the seconds ticked by. Each one seemed like an hour. This was supposed to be fast — a fatal interaction with the medication he took on a daily basis.

Something dawned on him. "What are you talking about? What have you done?" Ray tried to stand but he couldn't; he felt suddenly dizzy. The bitch couldn't have given him something, could she? His heart was fluttering now. He was losing it. Everything span around him. "What have you done to me?"

"What I should have had the courage to do years ago." Marilyn stood and slowly walked away. She turned to look back at him one last time.

Marilyn walked up to the warden, who was chatting with a young woman visitor.

"My husband is dying," she said simply.

He looked over towards Fallon just in time to see him hit the floor.

Suddenly there were people everywhere. A siren went off and someone led Marilyn away. She looked behind her and saw that the warden was trying to resuscitate Ray. It would do no good. He was dead.

Chapter 24

Sunday

"Apologies to you all for having to drag your sorry backsides in here on a Sunday. We're waiting for the Duggan, and then we can wrap this up. Where's Rocco?"

"The water people are putting the camera down that manhole at the back of the mill," Imogen told him. "He'll report back once they've had a thorough look."

At the very least Calladine was hoping they'd find Ron Weatherby. After that, he'd no idea what to expect.

Rhona Birch came into the office. "We have found a wealth of stuff on Chase's computer. He hasn't been exactly careful. A gift, is how one of the cyber team described it."

Calladine raised his coffee mug. "So it's building nicely. Good work, the lot of you."

"Sorry I'm late!"

It was Joyce.

"You didn't have to come in," Calladine told her. "I'm sorry, I should have said."

She took off her coat and sat down at her desk. "I'm here to co-ordinate everything you get today. You want this case sorted, so you need me." She logged on to her computer. "There is a new report on the system, from Professor Batho."

"What does it say?"

"Fingerprints on the locket match those belonging to Damien Chase!"

"Great news. With that, and the evidence on his computer, we have plenty to implicate him. He won't wriggle out of this. Pass me the phone. I'll ring him back."

"Give me a couple of hours and I'll have the results of the tissue from under Lauren Steele's fingernails. The rest you have, I presume."

"Yep. Thanks, Julian. See you later."

"Chase isn't happy, guv. He spent the night in the cells, despite his solicitor's best efforts to get him out."

"I'll speak to him again. Joyce, would you ring down and have him transferred to the interview room. Do you want to join me, Imogen?"

She nodded enthusiastically, grabbed her notebook and pen, and they walked down the stairs. "Looks like you've got him, sir. He can't possibly explain away all that stuff on his computer."

Chase was looking decidedly irritable. He was pulling a face as he sipped coffee from a plastic beaker.

"Poison! Bloody rubbish. I'll have to complain. The service around here is appalling. You do know that I play golf with the chief superintendent, don't you, Inspector?"

"Would that be Edwin Walker, Mr Chase?"

The man gave him a tight little smile and nudged his brief, who sat at his side.

"He's my uncle."

Calladine watched this sink in for a moment. "Now. We have your computer. There is a lot of extremely damning evidence on it."

"Nothing to do with me. I'm not the only person with access to it."

"I think you are. You see, it's password protected."

Chase whispered in Hughes's ear.

"Is that it? You put me through hell overnight and that's all you've got?"

"Not quite. Your fingerprints were found on a locket belonging to Lauren Steele, one of the bodies we've found. How do you explain that?"

Now it was Raymond Hughes's turn to look uncomfortable. "Anything to say, Mr Chase?" Calladine asked

"You are fitting me up."

"Is that the best you can do?"

There was a knock on the door and a uniformed officer entered. He handed Calladine a note. He studied it for a few seconds and then smiled. "Before Lauren was killed she fought with her assailant. She scratched him, hard. So hard it left traces of his tissue under her fingernails. The DNA extracted from that tissue is a match for yours, Mr Chase."

After more whispering, Hughes stood up. "I've advised my client to give you a full statement."

"But you can get me bail?"

"I don't think so, Damien. Not this time."

* * *

Imogen was almost skipping as they walked back to the office. "Don't you just love it when things come together like that?"

"Yes, but it takes a lot of work. Julian has done us proud."

"Rocco's been on," said Ruth. "They've found another body not far from the manhole entrance — male. Probably Ron Weatherby."

"Anything else?"

"Not yet. The water people say it could take weeks to search through all the tunnels, but they are going to give it a go."

"Good work all round."

"Professor Batho asked if you'd ring him, sir," said Joyce.

Calladine picked up the office phone. "Thanks, Julian. The results you produced nailed him. We have both Chase and Childers in the cells. They'll be up before the magistrate later today."

"I did find blood on the machete you took from Danny Newton's tent. It matched that of Snap Langton and Ron Weatherby. So there's your murder weapon for those two men, Tom. It was a blow to the back of the head that killed Newton, smashed his skull and wielded with force. Far more force than required to simply incapacitate someone."

"That's that, then. You joining us in the pub?"

"Now that I've finished working for you, yes — and you can buy the drinks."

* * *

Ruth had found them a table. "I don't think I can stay long. Jake's parking the car. He's all set for a session but I haven't got the energy."

"I said you were turning into a lightweight."

She threw a beer mat at him.

"Here's the doc and the rest of the team."

Rocco was gathering up extra chairs as Calladine greeted them.

"It's raining again," said Julian, as he and Tash came in.

"So, who's missing?"

"Amy?" said the doc.

"We're not an item anymore, I'm afraid." Calladine caught sight of the doc winking at Tash.

"So you're free again, Tom?"

"That's about it. Amy's doing a runner to Cornwall. I will miss her, but she doesn't do serious. She did warn me back at the beginning."

"Don't you have any influence, Julian?" said the doc.

The scientist cleared his throat and shook his head. Before he could reply, a voice spoke behind him.

"Mind if I join you?" said Birch. "Do you do this often?"

"Not often enough," the doc replied. "This crew are good. I miss working with them."

"I'll drink to that. That they're good, I mean. In fact I'll get a round in as a thank you. Care to give me a hand, Inspector? You know what everyone drinks."

Calladine accompanied her to the bar. This new Birch was almost as scary as the old one.

"There's something I have to tell you. When she left the station, Marilyn Fallon went directly to Strangeways, to visit her husband. During that visit she gave him something in a drink of water — a poison or medication, Digoxin, they think. Coming on top of the beta blockers he took, the effect was to make his heart stop."

Calladine didn't quite understand. "Is he in hospital? Is Marilyn okay?"

"Your cousin is dead, Inspector. The exact cause and the identity of the drug will be known once the post-mortem is done. Marilyn Fallon has been arrested."

"Dead . . ." For a moment he thought she might be joking but it wasn't her style. He smiled. "Marilyn finally did for him. I know I shouldn't, but all I can feel is an overwhelming sense of relief, like a huge weight has been lifted. That man has been a thorn in my side for as long as I can remember."

"Apparently so. I've been reading your file. I gather you were brought up together."

"He was my auntie Fran's boy. Auntie Fran did a runner when he was six. There was no father, so my mum took him in. She raised the pair of us together."

"His death lets you off the hook. No Fallon, no more need for witness protection. And Edwin Walker has been arrested."

That was a different story. Eve would be round, demanding answers, and he hadn't a clue what he was going to tell her.

"Before she left my office today, Marilyn gave me this to give to you. On reflection I should have realised she was going to do something, because she was rather cryptic about when I was to hand it over. She said I'd know when the time was right."

She handed him a pink, scented envelope. Calladine put it in his pocket.

"Thanks, ma'am. I'll read it later."

Birch practically downed her pint in one. "Go back and join your team. I'll see you on Monday."

"Did you see that?" said Ruth. "She made short work of that beer. She drinks like a bloke. She's not that bad though, is she, on balance? You have to admit, we've had worse."

Calladine had taken the pink envelope from his pocket and was opening it.

"That looks for all the world like a love letter. It smells like it too," said Ruth.

He scanned the contents. "It's from Marilyn." He read on, then gave a long slow whistle.

"What has she done?"

"She killed Fallon. Some sort of medication — a post-mortem will give the answer to that one. Whatever it was, it stopped his heart. But the icing on the cake, she's left me a file of all Fallon's wrongdoings. She writes that it contains names of those on his payroll, those he's used for the killings, the lot in fact."

"That's some parting gift. Poor woman. She must have had enough of turning a blind eye. He drove her to it. Where's she left this file?"

"She's sent it recorded delivery to my address. Can't wait," he smiled reading on. "Oh, and to top it off she wants me to have her dog! She's left it with a neighbour in the meanwhile and asks if I'll go pick it up."

"A dog might do you good, get you out walking. You might lose a bit of weight."

"Look who's talking!"

"I've got an excuse. You haven't."

Calladine called out to the group, "What sort of dog is a Shar Pei?"

"It's one of those wrinkly ones," said Imogen. "They can be quite cute."

"Well, that's what I'm taking on, and it's called Sam."

A lot of jokes followed, about doggy stuff and poo bags. The only one of them who had anything positive to say was Jake. He'd had a dog, which had died of old age at the beginning of the year. He'd been very attached to it.

Ruth gathered her stuff together and made to leave. "Monday will be my last day, Tom. I'll clear my desk and that'll be me gone for the duration. That means you'll have to speak to Lauren Steele's mum, I'm afraid."

"I'll sort it, don't worry." The others were chatting, baby stuff mostly, making arrangements to visit Ruth and keep in touch. Calladine felt miserable. Suddenly the day had gone flat. He couldn't bring himself to make small talk, crack jokes. He'd miss her too much.

Jake helped her up. Ruth did look enormous. It was high time she stopped working, particularly at this job. Calladine gave her a wistful smile and she patted his shoulder. No need for words. From this point forward their working lives would be changed forever.

THE END

Thank you for reading this book. If you enjoyed it please leave feedback on Amazon, and if there is anything we missed or you have a question about then please get in touch. The author and publishing team appreciate your feedback and time reading this book.

Our email is jasper@joffebooks.com

www.joffebooks.com

Made in the USA
San Bernardino, CA
24 May 2016